I0830413

Midnight in the Wilderness of America

MIDNIGHT IN THE WILDERNESS OF AMERICA.
Copyright © 2003, 2021 by Jordan Schniper. All rights reserved.
Printed in the United States of America. No part of this book
may be used or reproduced in any manner without written
permission from the author.

This is a work of fiction. All of the characters, organizations, and
events portrayed in this novel are either products of the author's
imagination or are used fictitiously.

ISBN: 978-0-692-17825-6

ABOUT THE AUTHOR

Jordan Schniper was born and raised in Alabama. He has a
BA in International Studies from Rhodes College in Memphis,
Tennessee, and an MBA from the University of Alabama at
Birmingham. He traveled to 46 states and half of America's
national parks while writing and researching the story. *Midnight
in the Wilderness of America* is his first novel, and will be his only
novel.

"The solar flares and auroras are scratching darkness across the surface of the Earth. Towers of Babel all across the world are going dormant. The technology inside them tumbling down."

Midnight in the Wilderness of America

BY

JORDAN SCHNIPER

HAWAII
VOLCANOES

Day 1

Midnight in the wilderness of Earth. Levi Wolff relaxes in a hammock under palm trees on a beach at the western edge of America. He stares into the distance where Kilauea's volcanic eruption bleeds through the jungle and circulates molten veins down a scorched landscape. Blazing lava flows to the edge of the island and collides with the ocean in a clash of elements that lifts smoke into the wind. Levi removes a letter from the pocket of his jeans and tilts the typed words into the glow of the moonlight.

> *A storm is coming. It is time to return home.*
> *Bring your blueprint with you. You need to hurry.*
> *There is a ticket waiting for you at the airport.*
> *Proceed to the coordinates on the back of this letter.*
> *Leave at dawn. And travel fast.*

He tucks the letter away and closes his eyes to rest for the journey that will ultimately take him back to the South. A season spent in tropical Hawaii removing invasive plant and animal species from parklands has ended. Now he is about to travel across a hard land haunted by the ghost of the American Dream.

Levi falls asleep thinking of an old legend dating back to the closing days of the Civil War. A Confederate raider named the CSS *Shenandoah* had sailed the waters around the Hawaiian Islands, attacking the Union whaling fleet and inflicting economic damage. When the war ended and the echo of *Shenandoah's* last shots faded away, the ship of a nation divided had circumnavigated the globe through a vast expanse of violence.

DEATH
VALLEY

Day 2

The plane that rose in Kona at daylight's break touches down in San Diego midday. Levi walks out of the airport and hails a taxi. He places a duffel bag of clothes and backpack of personal items on the seat beside him and gives instructions to an address on the outskirts of town. Then he slips into silence and slides sunglasses down over his eyes as the coast fades away and the cab winds into urban sprawl.

Thirty minutes later they arrive at the gates of a storage facility, across the street from a fire station and supermarket. He pays the driver cash. As the cab rolls away he reaches into the collar of his shirt and lifts a dog tag chain necklace that holds a silver Star of David and two keys. Levi unclasps the necklace and the keys slide off into the palm of his hand. He tucks both keys into the back pocket of his jeans, picks up his bags and walks under a blazing sun among the concrete storage rows until he reaches a unit in the middle. There he retrieves one of the keys and unlocks the deadbolt. He slides the large door up along its hinges and flips the light switch on.

The storage unit contains only one item. A fully stocked

matte black 4x4 hardtop pickup truck. Levi moves around the vehicle inspecting it. Air pressure in the ribbed off road tires still good. The backseat and floorboards still filled with jerrycans of fuel and boxes of liquor and tobacco, to barter with. Everything seeming intact he removes the second key from his pocket and unlocks the back tailgate. Inside, a memory foam bed and stacks of clothes are horseshoed by three metal long boxes running along the sides and back of the cab. Levi climbs in and checks each of the boxes that contain survival supplies, food, water, cash, silver and gold coins, guns and ammo.

Levi tosses the duffel bag and backpack on the bed, secures the tailgate, then unlocks the driver door. When he slides into the driver seat, his pulse quickens. He tries to slow the beat of his heart with lengthy exhales. There is no margin for error. No time for delays and repairs. A clock is ticking and Levi knows he needs to hurry and create distance. He inserts the key into the ignition and waits a long second, staring out the windshield through the storage unit door into the sunshine and concrete lane that will connect him to the long road home. Levi turns the key and the engine cranks and purrs to life after three months of hibernation.

He puts the truck in gear and drives out of the storage unit. Two miles down the road he enters an on ramp to the interstate and leaves the coastal city behind, heading northeast along I-15. He navigates the grid of a parched land with the radio on and windows rolled down. Outlaw country songs become his passenger. The city fades. Agricultural countryside appears alongside warehouses, wind farms, and nearly finished desalinization plants constructed to replenish freshwater aquifers. Levi drives for hours until the setting sun melts on the desert horizon and a dry wind fills the cabin.

He exits the interstate past Barstow, moving onto rural highway. Headlights from his rumbling truck tunneling deep into the barren desert. He passes into a frontier zone of lonely highway stretching further into the night. The standard green mile marker signs of the American road fade to sun baked blue signs. The land empty except for a brief cluster of glowing light from a supermax prison.

Static creeps in over the radio so he changes the station. Halfway through a song, shrill emergency beeps cut the music. A slow mechanical voice follows.

"This is a message from the Emergency Broadcasting System. An X-class geomagnetic solar storm is striking Asia. America has lost contact with that region of the world. Citizens are advised to stay tuned to regular news updates."

The message concludes with more klaxon beeps as punctuation. Levi absorbs the information, again feeling his heart rate quicken. The storm he was forewarned about in the letter has arrived. He turns the tuning nob to other stations with human voices.

. . .

"The lights are about to go out in some of the most densely populated places on Earth. It will be a long time before they turn on again. And by then the world will be a different place."

. . .

"America's Armed Forces are raising the Defcon alert and going into defensive posture."

. . .

"Sources we have talked to say there is genuine concern that the impacted countries could unleash electromagnetic pulse bombs in skies over other continents to level the balance of power."

. . .

"We are now in the orbit of chaos."

. . .

"It just hit the wire. Ghost ships are clogging the Straits of Malacca. Egypt is sealing the Suez Canal. The Strait of Gibraltar and Panama Canal could be next. Then the airports."

. . .

"With more people living in cities than the countryside for the first time in human history, this could be the most dangerous event since World War II."

. . .

"What is this thing?" a caller asks.

"Electrically charged shockwaves from space," the radio host explains, "A natural phenomena of solar wind that can collide with Earth's atmosphere as the planet turns on its axis."

. . .

Levi flips to more radio stations. Same reports. Different words. Same meaning. He tightens his grip on the steering wheel and remembers that the word "news" is a forgotten acronym for north, east, west and south. Cardinal directions of a compass now shrinking inward in scope.

A strange calm develops within him. Survival instinct. The realization that every decision, every step, from this moment forward, is precious and holds consequences. A familiar feeling for so many months in so many places during the past year on the road. He speeds up. Pavement carries him deeper into the star lit desert as he processes the impact of the solar flare.

The death of electricity. Technology zones shattered. Entire storehouses of digital data and knowledge wiped clean. Primitive and outdated modes suddenly back in style. He realizes more storms could be on the way, causing a power vacuum in the echo of darkness as solar flares move through the Milky Way galaxy's Orion arm like sepsis. A new dark age arriving with the whirlwind.

On the outskirts of Death Valley Junction, he exits the road to fill up the gas tank. He drives past a "Buy American" billboard with a graffiti mural depicting Wall Street wizards in dunce caps mixing a cauldron of toxic brew for a breadline wrapping around a city block.

Levi enters a massive truck stop functioning as a mini city.

On the edge of the parking lot, an employee perches on a ladder at the illuminated gas price sign taking down old numbers and raising new ones, announcing that times are changing.

He parks in front of a fuel pump ringed by dozens of eighteen wheelers and climbs out into air that carries a foul stench from nearby slaughterhouses. Levi feeds $5 bills into a slot and gas begins to flow while he eyes a truck wash at the back of the lot, where cabs are lined up to remove the grime of the long haul. Cars exit the highway and idle while they wait their turn at the pumps. A palpable vibe of urgency from the news.

After filling up Levi frees his spot at the pump and parks in the back of the lot below a tall light pole craning a flickering orange bulb. He locks his truck and walks through the big rigs to enter a rest stop split between a modern food mart and an old fashioned diner, where waitresses hustle among the booths, and short order cooks call out ticket numbers as they slide comfort food onto the counter. He walks through the area and down a long hallway, past a wall of pay phones, a gambling arcade, and locker room with showers, to the restroom. Then he returns to the mart to buy a bag of sunflower seeds and fill a cup with a roast of strong coffee.

Outside, he sips the hot coffee on the walk back to his truck through the grid of tractor trailers marked by airbrushed art on the cabs and stamped with corporate logos stretching down the trailers. He nears the back of the lot and pavement gives way to gravel that grinds underfoot with each step. The narrow lanes contain a nocturnal subculture that moves among the sleep deprived drivers. A bleach blond prostitute up ahead knocks on the door of a produce truck to little avail. She glances down at Levi as he walks by and opens a mouth smeared with bright pink lipstick. "Hey there, sugar." Levi smiles politely and shakes his head to rescind the offer as he passes by.

He makes a few more turns, walks a few more lanes until

he spots his truck. Beside it, a man with penitentiary muscles is leaning against the light pole, the bulb above burning in and out with strobe effect.

Levi feels the glazed skid row eyes sizing him up and cracks his toes inside his cowboy boots in anticipation. Knowing that in a street fight he needs to hit first. Quick and vicious to improve the odds.

The man steps off the pole and walks forward to meet Levi at the edge of the maze of trucks.

"Hey bud, how bout a boost for the road?" The lanky dealer's crocodile smile reveals yellow rotting teeth and infected gums. "I've got speed, crank, grass, and a whole bunch of pills just waitin' to slide on down."

Levi senses danger coming like a Juarez sunset. He stops six feet from the man. "Not interested."

"Well then." The dealer reaches into a pocket and taps a baggie of powder. "This is new. It's called Mindcrawler. You heard of it yet? You will. It's a new realm. Sixty dollars to take it for a spin."

Anger swelling, Levi holds up his coffee. "I'm all set, man. Like I said. Not interested."

The drifter scratches at a tat on his forearm. Then runs his hand through long slick hair. "Then how bout a ride to the next town?" He starts to extend a hand. "My name is Wayne."

"Not a chance. I'm traveling solo."

Wayne nods and sniffs, drawing air into his sinuses. "Do you know what's about to happen?"

"I'm a little slow," Levi replies. "Speed it up for me."

"You're going to drop the keys," Wayne warns as he balls his hands into fists and steps forward. "And then you're going to run."

Reflexes instant, Levi pushes aside the fear of being robbed and stranded, channeling adrenalin as he sloshes his coffee into the dealer's face and quickly closes the distance between them. Wayne's slick grin vanishes as he cusses in pain and wipes away the burning coffee. Before the man can reset, Levi delivers a vicious cowboy boot kick into the solar plexus. The dealer drops to his knees and gasps for air. A honed knee to the face crushes bone.

Levi lifts Wayne by the hair, walks him across the lane and slams the stranger's head against the side of a semi-trailer. The wrecked body lands in a heap on the gravel. Levi takes his boot and stomps the ribs until he hears a crunch. Then he uses the dealer's broken rib cage as traction to roll the body under the trailer.

Walking lane cleared, Levi looks around in the solemn shadows to see if anyone spotted the fight in the back alley of the truck stop. Nothing. Just people moving through the night, going about their business. Levi takes one last look around the complex and blight. Then he climbs into his truck and slowly drives out, past a hitchhiker with facial tattoos waiting on the edge of the highway ramp. He rejoins the road, heading deeper into the desert.

An hour later, Levi enters a small unincorporated area on the border of Death Valley National Park called Nomad Junction. He drives through the run down town and brakes as two bales of tumbleweed blow across the road and bounce off a chain link fence next to a fast food restaurant. A pale tweaker with a corpse like face peers out from behind a dumpster with a bag of discarded food in his hand before disappearing back into the shadows.

Levi drives on through an intersection with a solitary yellow blinking traffic light swinging on a power line like an effigy, and finishes his approach to a lime colored motel of single story rooms laid out in a semicircle. The place abandoned except for a silver pickup truck parked in front of the office.

He parks and walks by the Broken Spur Motel sign framed by flickering yellow bulbs buzzing as if they are roasting bugs on their filaments. He enters the office cautiously, closes the rickety door, and waits for the bell above the frame to stop ringing. A night manager with a cowboy hat tucked low over his brow sits on a stool behind the counter reading a newspaper and listening to faint voices fading in and out of the static on an AM radio station. A canvas satchel rests beside him on the counter.

"I have an argot reservation under the name Clive W. Hart." Levi places a patch from Hawaii Volcanoes National Park on the counter to unlock the conversation.

The night manager lowers his newspaper and peers up with the look of a gunslinger who has no feeling in his trigger finger. Crows feet wrinkles etch the corners of dark brown eyes. Dusty blond hair pokes out from beneath the cowboy hat whose brim lays a shadow across a patch of burned skin on his jaw.

"Did you bring your updated paradigm?"

Levi reaches into a pocket of his jeans and places folded papers on the counter. Then takes a pen and signs the top of the papers with his left hand.

The man picks the pages up and reads for a long moment while Levi listens to the radio emissions.

"Any changes since Alaska?"

"A few. Nothing significant."

The night manager nods slightly and stands, slipping the pages into the satchel. Then places a patch from Shenandoah National Park on the counter that holds the image of a black bear roaming the woods. "I'm Outlander. The new sheriff of Shenandoah. If I can get there." He pauses to gather his things. "We need to go. I imagine you've heard the news by now."

"Yes."

"Did they tell you anything about the plan?"

"No, just to be here at these coordinates as soon as possible."

"National park lodges are about to become a network of neutral ground for government employees on missions. The shelf life for a modern city without electricity is thirty days. Too many trajectories and unknowns in a city if its power grid goes down. We need sanctuaries that insulate us. There will be time to talk further down the road." Outlander peers through the window at Levi's truck. "Stay focused and try to block out distractions. The price of scorpion venom in Katmandu is of no concern to you." He places the motel keys on the counter and walks towards the door. "Follow me and keep close."

"Aren't you gonna lock up?"

"Nah. These keys are for whoever wants this place. This town is finished."

Out in the parking lot the sheriff unlocks the door to his truck and hands Levi a grey bulletproof vest. "We will need to wear these as a uniform for access to the outposts and to resupply along the way."

Levi spots a patch on the left side of the vest above the heart that reads SECRET EDEN in black letters against a yellow background.

"Your Shenandoah patch will be sewn on the right side. But there will be time for that later. Let's go."

They climb into their pickup trucks and pull out of the motel parking lot, round a corner, and two blocks down, enter an on ramp. Yellow lines of highway paint stream into darkness along phantom roads as they move through empty land, away from the pandemonium that will soon occur in the mega cities and along the borderlands. When they cross the state line into Arizona, the road widens and slabs of interstate march on the long road home. Levi and Outlander drive all night until the sun begins to rise and the sky lightens with dawn as dust devils twirl along the frontier.

PETRIFIED FOREST

Day 3

Levi sits on the tailgate of his truck at a rest stop outpost along the Eisenhower grid in Thirsty Cactus, Arizona, sipping on a sarsaparilla soda as he sews the Shenandoah patch on his vest. State troopers guard the main area, open to the public, while out back National Guard soldiers stake tents on open ground that is converting into bivouac barracks. A Cold War design that had been lying fallow now fully awake.

Across the road to the north, a vacant demolition derby arena's hijacked marquee sign reads words of stacked stone.

The Tower Void
princes will gather when the stars bleed
to battle the severed branches for thrones of power
the 13th zodiac will tear the feathers from a fallen eagle
and set upon the loose bands who quiver in an unbound darkness

Levi looks away from the cold omen to a mile south in the Painted Desert where stumps of petrified wood are strewn among winding mounds of badlands formations layered with alternating hues of sediment. He finishes sewing the patch and hops down, walking past the grill of his truck that has become a canvas of splattered bugs marked by pellets of yellow, brown and red juice.

Outlander returns from resupplying their fuel and they sit atop a picnic bench, digging into their rations.

"So how long were you based out of that motel in Death Valley?"

"Not long. I spent most of my time around the Salton Sea."

"Oh." Levi had passed by there once, briefly. The slender trailers and houses looked like a bunch of giant crayons dumped into a ghost town beside a poisoned lake.

Outlander puts a hand crank emergency radio down on the table and changes the subject. "I spoke to the camp commander who is getting secure channel intercepts. The American military is pulling back from overseas bases and returning home. Troops and equipment are already in route."

"It's speeding up isn't it?"

"Yes. We need to move faster. Much faster."

They pack up their food and are about to climb into their trucks when an old school bus pulls up and sputters into the parking lot like a tired hornet. An elderly man with a white beard and faded ball cap pulls the folding doors open and calls to them. "You fellas got any spare gas? I'm from the local youth home. I'm trying to get these youngsters to safety."

They survey the old man in his grease stained overalls. Then glance to the bus windows where little kids press their innocent faces to the glass as they lift their tiny hands to wave. Levi and Outlander wave back.

"Where you heading, sir?" Outlander asks.

"East. Twenty miles from here. The town isn't safe. I'm taking them out to the mayor's ranch."

Levi looks over at Outlander. "How many canisters you got?"

"Three. How bout you?"

"Two."

Outlander nods. "Hold up. I got one for you." He reaches into the back cab of his truck and walks a jerrycan to the fuel tank beside the doors of the old school bus to refill the nearly empty bin. When Outlander finishes, the driver gets out of his seat to shake hands with them as two police cars with lights lit up race by, heading west.

"Thank you, young men. Mighty kind of you."

"Glad to help." Outlander taps the side of the school bus. "Travel safe."

They watch the nearly beaten bus groans its way down the road and disappear from view.

The two travelers reach the Arizona-New Mexico state line at noon and make a brief pit stop at a dimly lit cinder block saloon for a cold beer and bowl of hatch chili. When they rejoin the road the sun is riding high in the sky. Levi rolls his windows down and keeps his eyes on the silver pickup truck ahead of him, aware of his silhouette riding the ground over cactus and shrub as they travel east. The shadow and the breeze glide his thoughts to the year of wandering it took to heal the wounds of a near-death experience.

Marked for death because of an idea typed in indigo ink on an old Corona folding typewriter. A logic of simplicity to remove the construct of complexity. A potential blueprint for the survival of America's economy. Research on the need for a new model that merges environmental, economic and strategic challenges into a unified field theory that benefits all citizens instead of just the elite. Research that ultimately made him a man on the run who disappeared off the grid to survive.

Before everything changed, he was living in rural Alabama. Working construction during the day while attending graduate school at night. He took his thesis to a conference in Montgomery for a dry run. Stood in front of a projector in a suit and tie in a room full of strangers and presented his idea. A sustainable tangible currency paradigm. Liberty dollars to replace globalist fiat money.

That night he went with friends to hear an 80s cover band play at a bar overlooking the Alabama River. It was a good night until a man in black passed by. Tan with Mediterranean features who moved easily among the crowd. The stranger stopped to ask Levi the name of the band. Stayed only for a moment. And moved on.

While Levi was distracted by looking over at the band as he answered the stranger's question, his beer was spiked with a tablet of exotic poisons that quickly dissolved in the foam and liquid. Neurotoxins began to take hold. By the time he finished the pale ale, the effects were already burrowing into the subconsciousness of his mind. Fever, toxic delirium, and hallucinations followed. The border between life and death became unclear as he left the bar and his friends in silence and wandered along the river walk before vomiting uncontrollably and rolling down a hill into a coma on the side of the river.

When Levi woke in the hospital days later he was visited by a retired judge from the Florida panhandle.

"You are lucky to be alive. Had your body not reacted so violently to the drugs, you woulda kept them down and died."

Levi just stared at him.

"It was also good that you didn't go to your truck that night. They were waiting for you just in case. You woulda disappeared."

"Who is *they*?"

"Elusive men who are fixers for powerful people who have relocated to the Gulf Coast. The kind of people who live on yachts and remove people from equations that harm their interests." The judge takes a piece a paper from the pocket of his sport coat and puts on reading glasses. "In your case, by delivering a potent blend of Caribbean poisons sourced from the swamps of the Arawak jungle. Datura stramonium, puffer fish tetrodotoxin, buga toad venom, sea snake gland, and ground seeds from toxic plants. A wide range of pH values in the potion you ingested. So rare to show up on a toxicology report that is sends a certain kind of message to you and anyone who was planning on funding your research." The judge looks up at Levi. "No one will want to get within a mile of your thesis project now."

"I don't know what half that stuff is." Levi looks out the window of his hospital room, across a grass lawn leading down to a waters edge and watches a postman delivering mail by boat to boxes on the dock. Bird feeders dangle from the branches of old oaks all around the yard. Nearby a hummingbird hovers to drink nectar before gliding away with majestic speed. "Where am I?"

"Magnolia Springs. We moved you down river. You were admitted under a different name."

Levi continues to stare out the window into blue skies and sunshine.

"You are still in danger. They will send others."

"It's just an idea, man. I don't even know if it will work. That is why I was asking for a grant to test the state of Alabama as a model. A framework that could also be applied to other states."

The judge rises from the chair, places the toxicology report on Levi's hospital bed and walks to the window where he watches a bright red cardinal chirp and dart from a tree branch to grab a mouthful of seed. "A viable formula that sunsets fiat money and derivatives futures trading in order to shift to tangibles will upend trillions of dollars' worth of embedded financial power as well as coveted political power. An unnatural perpetual deficit fueled power that threatens the Constitution." He turns from the window to face Levi. "Now that you are awake. You need to leave and go far. The doctors cleared you for travel."

"Where will I go?"

"You are being offered a new identity and work in America's

national parks as a seasonal employee so that you can continue your research in the field."

"And if I say yes?" Levi asks.

"Then we will help you liquidate your possessions so that you can pay off your student loans and any other debt. Your truck has already been painted a different color and been given a new license plate. If you say yes then you will need to change plates and names each new state in order to blend in."

"Is my truck here outside?"

The judge shakes his head. "No, your truck is with your family. They are at a house in Seagrove Beach waiting for your decision. And to say goodby. A temporary goodbye. If you say yes, we will move them out of the city and protect them too."

"I don't know what to do." Levi closes his eyes. "I need time to think."

"I need your answer by sundown." The judge sighs, "We are all sired by circumstance, Levi. The question is what path you will choose. If you stay they will hunt you down for sport. If you drive away you head into the unknown."

That night the judge returned. Levi met him at the door and gave his answer. On the drive east over to Seagrove they had time to talk.

"When you don't know what to do out there just find shelter someplace safe and try to sleep to recharge. Things are often clearer the next day," he advises. "Revere the wild places you will go and watch your six."

"You haven't even told me your name," Levi asked before the judge drove away.

"Mahlon. Judge Mahlon Emmett."

Levi spent that night at the beach with his parents and siblings. The next morning he loaded up and headed further south into Florida, opposite of the direction he felt his new enemies would expect, driving the islands along the Keys. He parked his truck at the Key West airport and hopped a float plane to an isolated fort in the ocean, where for the next month he helped repair brick walls at Dry Tortugas National Park. Waking in the middle of the night from bad dreams that seemed to sever his tanned body from his disheveled spirit. Free but scared. Missing home. Alive but wounded on a level that medicine could not track, or fix. Only time and distance and deep breathes of fresh air could provide the antidote to heal him.

During that month at Tortuga, he began to cull his boxed library of books down to just the Torah, the Constitution, and a blank leather travel journal. Levi scanned every other book from his library. A library that he viewed as a gathering of minds throughout time. Folding down the corners of the pages that held something he might want to recall. Then breaking the spine of the book. Recycling the discarded pages or burning them in small campfires on the narrow sandbar beach at night. Lifting quotes and facts of distilled knowledge from the bent pages into the esoteric travel journal.

In his lifetime he was witness to the death of journalism and the theft of the American Dream. Levi Wolff was not ready to pick up his blueprint yet. But he began to prepare for the day that he would.

Levi returned to the mainland and drove along the seaports of the Atlantic Coast, taking the scenic route, choosing backroads over interstates, steering clear of cities and skid row districts. Keeping to himself and moving campgrounds every few days. Ending up in Congaree National Park in South Carolina where he helped repair boardwalks in the swamps of the old growth forest. At night in the woods he began parking his pickup truck pointed at the North Star, the way cowboys would orient the wagon train in the frontier days to help them navigate to the next destination.

He crossed the Mason-Dixon line and left his regional culture behind. Adapting his restless soul to that of a wanderer.

Embracing being a minimalist with few possessions and freedom of movement. He was living life to a different rhythm as a nomad in places where the days run long and tranquil.

Levi moved on up into Maine and followed the Aroostook River along fishing wharves and arrived in Acadia National Park to work on a maintenance crew. During his down time he walked through the white birch tree woods and old colonial paths for hours along the calm harbors. Many mornings, starting at Sand Beach and climbing the Beehive granite slabbed rock hill where he could stare out along the woodland and coastal waters dotted with the granite humps of small islands. The surf and sea spray along the rugged shore shook loose whispers of memory of what it felt like to be happy. Even on the stormy days when the ocean rolled its surface, rising and falling and tossing with a swell of waves. And some nights he would drive into Bar Harbor and grab a lobster roll and a frothy beer in a chilled mug at the Bangor Cave Speakeasy and listen to a lounge singer's seductive voice sing authentic blues songs from the Mississippi Delta in French lyrics that floated over the room like a trance.

Eventually Levi left the Lower 48 and moved up into Canada and drove the wide roads all the way west to the Tok Junction and into an Alaskan border town in the Last Frontier. He camped behind a trading post up the road from an old silver mine on the border of Wrangell National Park. Lived in a tiny enclave surrounded by tall snow capped mountains lining the distant horizon like sharp teeth. Obtained a subsistence permit and fished the swift glacier fed waters of the Copper River for king, sockeye, and silver salmon that held adaptogens of extra fat and essential oils built for the long journey upriver, where the fish spawned and died to nourish their offspring. Levi felt at peace in the vast wilderness of sitka and spruce trees and dark blue lakes. Especially when the ethereal Aurora Borealis would flare in the atmosphere and aqua green ion waves glided across the night sky with a low whistle in the air that soothed his soul.

Levi left Wrangell National Park the morning of the first cold rain as the seasons began to change and before the frozen isolation of winter appeared. He passed by a Thai food truck painted bright purple and a line of idle snow machines at the junction and continued west along the Alaska Highway. He stayed on Highway 1 through Anchorage, following the cut of the road alongside train tracks and the sea, through marsh fields and past steep mountains dotted with the orange leaves of Aspen trees. Detouring at Girdwood, down a long stretch of unpaved road pock marked with dirt holes to the Crow Creek gold mining camp, where it felt like stepping back through time. He camped for a week beside an old surplus World War II Alaskan Command truck with a snarling polar bear logo, its polished chrome grill attached to a fading navy blue cab losing a battle to rust and time. Waking each morning at the edge of camp to bathe at the bank of a cold rushing river that seemed more suited for kayaking than fortune hunting.

Levi continued down the peninsula and parked at Exit Glacier in Kenai Fjords National Park where the Alaskan twilight lingered, its soft blue spectrum entombed in a frozen river's deep crevices like forged cobalt glass. The blue ice matching the color of his eyes.

During the day he would hike along the fields where the glacier's slow retreat thawed a wide flow of thin water across a dark field of smooth rock. A process that had been underway since the Civil War, long before the machines of man spread into a remote land, that is now a state whose border connects to the Bering Strait, that was once the Bering Land Bridge. And at night beside a campfire he would watch the moon rise, its orb entering a star filled sky. At times he wondered how much the spike in global population and relentless march of civilization was speeding up the process of emerging from an Ice Age.

He took a job on a boat in Seward harbor that led sailing tours through the Gulf of Alaska. Abundant wildlife all around. Bald eagles and puffins nesting in the lush fjords and flying about. Seals gathered and flopping around on the wet rocks. Dahl dolphins with their skin marked black on top and white on bottom like miniature killer whales, surfacing alongside the boat, darting and cutting, before veering off and disappearing into the ocean blue.

Levi continued his pattern of moving often, loaded up, and drove out of town heading back up Alaska Highway 1. Veering off at Portage's glacier gripped mountains where a rock bored tunnel led to a former secret government town. The tunnel to the town of Whittier on the other side passing by giant rectangular safe house doors reserved for nuclear fallout. At Whittier he booked passage on a ship for him and his truck on a route along the Alaskan Maritime Highway that would deposit him in Washington and back in the Lower 48.

He drove slowly to new places that passed time, that drifted into weeks and months. Each new destination holding a unique beauty and aspect of American culture. Seeking out overgrown graveyards in shuttered lumber mill towns, ripping new identities off tombstones. Each new park providing a lily pad of temporary work. His travels took him deeper into the west until he was riding a tongue of road rising and falling across a high desert landscape of juniper trees and scraggy red earth. A yellow line leading to a town in the distance residing below a tall mountain pyramiding up into the sky.

After working on a maple tree farm in Bend, Levi spent time in Crater Lake National Park clearing brush and helping forest rangers perform controlled burns. Until one clear night he stood atop the rim of the extinct volcano and watched the sky float its reflection of blazing stars on the cold still water. He thought about the invisible lines of the ecliptic orbit carving a Zodiac line through space that snakes between 30 to 60 degrees latitude. The same design down on Earth that connects the world's most powerful capitals as a mirror upon the galaxy. The dual images, one seen, one unseen, stirred something deep in him and he decided keep in motion to outrun the strange forces that had put him on his journey.

His biorhythms were different than they were before the coma. During the day he was normal and outgoing. But at night his creativity unlocked and he became introverted. Levi left Oregon and took a long drive down through California, traveling across fault lines of sustainability, where he rented a storage shed and took two bags with him as he flew to Hawaii nine months into healing on the road. A sense of purpose reforming as he started to work on his research again upon arrival.

WHITE
SANDS

Day 4

Levi wakes at dawn in the Tularosa Basin and climbs out of the back of his truck. Beside him, Outlander is scanning the horizon of the alkali flat where a man on stilts walks along the vast gypsum sand dunes like a giraffe, holding a rifle and tracking through the ocular scope. They watch red tracer bullets spear from the rifle and speed across the New Mexico desert towards targets.

"What's going on?"

"That's Echo out there. The sheriff of Great Sand Dunes National Park in Colorado." Outlander points. "There was an infiltration last night." He hands Levi a pair of binoculars. "Scan to the right of Echo."

Levi looks through the binoculars at the rolling dunes of white sand and spots crimson blotches of gore where slain intruders scatter the slope of a dune, their ruptured torsos resembling busted piñatas.

"Did you get some sleep?" Outlander asks him.

"Yeah. Some."

"Good because we need to move. Echo woke me in the

middle of the night. Los Angeles and Seattle have gone dark. They were hit by high altitude EMPs launched from a submarine and frigate in the Pacific Ocean."

Levi hands the binoculars back and watches an electric dawn paint the sky.

"Echo is leading a convoy north today that is being routed up to the grasslands of the High Plains to retro fit the electric water pumps that tap into the Ogallala Aquifer." Outlander motions to a motorcycle nearby leaning on a kick stand, stocked with saddlebags on each side of the rider seat. "That vast underground lake of freshwater is what sustains the Breadbasket. The pumps need a manual option to withdraw the water if the electricity goes out to help prevent another Dust Bowl." Outlander reaches into his coat pocket and lifts an envelope. "And this classified overseas report arrived from command at the nearby missile range. The news is not good."

"What does it say?"

"You're gonna have to make it further down the road before you have that kind of clearance."

Outlander goes silent, thinking about the chance to stop off and visit his family's farm in the Cumberland Gap on the way to Shenandoah. A year ago when he last visited, his parents and sisters treated him as if he had been there all along, a gift to him that they had yet to realize had been given. He had moved away over two decades ago, ever since the urge to see other places had taken him away from a small town and onto domestic battlefields defined by skirmishes in the shadows of the underworld, often supervised out of windowless situation rooms with complex screens. He longed for the stillness of the farm with its soothing pace of life a thousand miles away. The woman he loves, even closer.

Fatigue from a restless night of sleep rolls over him and stings his vision. A final season of government work and then he will let go. Regardless of the tasks that remain, Outlander vows to quit when the obligation is fulfilled. Then he can live the quiet life with his future wife in the place he had once spent so much time dreaming about leaving. Pickup trucks parked in drive-ins. Country roads to race across. Crops and rows of corn to fill the horizon with signs of bounty. Hard rains and soft music. Country diners and sunburned farmers. Quaint churches and house porches. Fall football in the fields and winter basketball in the gyms. It would be a good life to return to. If any of it is left after the fallout from the Aurora Terra.

"Levi, we have a seek and destroy stop to make along the way in Texas. An outlaw motorcycle gang is holed up and could threaten the outposts in nearby national parks. They're wanted dead or alive."

"Which gang?"

"The Armadillos. I patched in with them while I was undercover back then operating under the street name of Wicked Will Baraboo." Outlander's dark brown eyes carrying a glean of mayhem. "That cover identity was retired. But I'm going to bring it back one last time."

"Baraboo? What kind of name is that?"

"It's a rural town in Wisconsin that minted rodeo clowns back in the day."

They load up and a few minutes later their trucks speed across the wide desert landscape, intersect with a strip of asphalt and swing right, heading east, away from the giant sandbox.

TALLGRASS

Day 5

Prairie spans a horizon dotted with oil rigs bobbing into the dry ground like large steel locusts while white clouds tumble across a pale blue Comanche county sky. Levi and Outlander pull off on the shoulder of a desolate two lane country highway below the I-20 corridor, and cut their engines. A mile up, a dusty path, flanked by golden fields of tallgrass on each side, leads to a compound with a row of motorcycles parked in front a tough saloon.

Outlander climbs out of his truck, grabs a dock kit from the backseat, and moves to the tailgate to get ready. He recalls the saloon's raspy jukebox near the billiards tables. The worn couches of the clubhouse. White powder residue on the table tops. A vault below the floorboards to store guns, drugs, and money. The brothel cabins out back. And the smell of barbecue smoke from the grill riding the wind.

"Wait here. Have your AR-15 at the ready. I'm about to go stomp on a den of rattlesnakes." Outlander unzips the dock kit and removes the tops from different colored canisters, dips his fingers in and uses a small handheld mirror to apply face paint until he looks like a crazed rodeo clown. Then he draws two long yellow teeth on the corners of his mouth that look like the tusks of an inverted bone mustache.

Levi stares at the menacing specter of Outlander's transformation into Will Baraboo. "Man, what kind of sheriff are you?"

"The banished kind. Just someone who comes out of the shadows to lend assistance and then returns to the shadows." Outlander ties a blue bandana around his neck and grins under the mask. "But the frontier breed are back in style." He tucks a pistol into the small of his back and takes a gun belt, lassos it to his hips, and puts two orange flare guns into each holster. "You'd be surprise what one of these suckers can do to the cab of a pickup truck or a rider on the open road when bad things go down at 80 miles an hour."

"What if you don't come back?"

"Then high tail it out of here. The judge is expecting you. The men up there killed my partner and have a bounty on my head. While I'm gone get these trucks turned around on the opposite site of the road and hitch them together. If I make it back I'll be inbound towin' some mean freight. Gradually slow roll 'em within a quarter mile."

Outlander slips a backpack over his shoulders and walks down the rural highway, his profile growing smaller across the slow mile. He reaches the entrance gate and recognizes two bouncers sitting on bar stools under the shade of drought stricken mesquite trees running up both sides of the driveway.

"Wicked Will Baraboo. We thought you were dead." Zeke rises and spits a stream of brown tobacco juice from the wad of dip tucked under his lip and casually scrapes at the ground with a worn Louisville slugger baseball bat. "Where you been this past year?" Zeke's jowls grinning while he stands there looking like a dromedary with a hump gut. Big and mean. Sly and cruel.

"I got some distance from that mess. Rode around until I caught a sheet up in Bozeman, Montana in a bar fight. Apparently bear spraying a bunch of drunk loggers who jump you in a parking lot is a felony. Worked road crew the better part of a year. It wasn't so bad all things considered. At least the scenery was good."

Kevin, a bare knuckle mauler with a mean streak and steroid fueled chorded muscles steps off his stool with a sawed off shotgun pointed to the side. His pale blue eyes taking the visitor's measure. "Well, the club will decide that. Come on in, Will. You're still a patched in Armadillo. They'll be glad to see you." His close cropped blond hair and mutton chop sideburns blurring into the sunshine while his eyes lock in a stare that is a dare. "Garret, Silas, Darien. They're all up there. Even the Detroit Reaper."

Outlander considers the words. "I don't think so, Kevin. Tell them to come meet me at the road and to leave the glue sniffers behind." Kevin starts to speak. Outlander holds up a hand. "In a minute." Outlander looks to Zeke, sun in his eyes and grit in his voice. "You still preying on teen runaways at Greyhound bus stations?"

Zeke's jaw muscles tighten and he shakes his head to shrug off the insult. "The way things went down with Porter Draw was a regrettable situation. But all things pass. Come on up, Baraboo. Enough with the sass."

Outlander lifts one of the orange flare guns from the holster with his left hand in a fast smooth motion and fires a shell into Zeke's gut as his right hand removes the pistol from the small of his back to get the drop on Kevin. "Don't raise that shotgun."

Zeke's big belly lights up like a jack o'lantern and he drops to the ground, hollering and rolling around like a fat evil pumpkin.

"I shoulda plugged you with buckshot you the moment you walked through the gate," Kevin says as veins stand out on his neck.

Outlander smirks under the mask of rodeo clown face paint. "Kevin, go on up and get 'em before I put a bullet in your knee." Zeke's screams fade as he passes out from the pain while his skin and clothes smolder. Kevin's eyes flare as he tosses the short barrel shotgun into the dirt. "Three... Two..."

Kevin turns and starts running up the long dirt road to the clubhouse. He looks back once and Outlander points his gun. Kevin obeys and runs faster. When Kevin has cleared a hundred yards, Outlander pulls the bandana up over his mouth and nose. Then lifts his other flare gun towards the canopy of mesquite trees flanking the path and shoots a large flaming slug. Drought had turned the trees into giant matches and now they have their spark. Fire spreads and when a concealing smoke lifts into the wind across the parched wilderness, Outlander slips his backpack off and works quickly.

He ties a strand of concertina piano wire to a burning tree and runs the wire across the road and ties it off on another tree. Then reaches down and grabs a handful of brown dirt that he rubs along the length of the wire to take the shine off. He hears the rumble of motorcycle engines cranking and looks up to the compound in the distance and spots a mob emptying out of the saloon. Motors from jet black bikes and an apple red eighteen wheeler roaring in approach. Men lining up to die.

Outlander grabs his pack and jogs back to the highway, stopping just past the corrugated tubes of a cattle grate. He dips into the backpack and uncurls a steel strip of highway patrol tire spikes across the ground. Trap set, he kicks some dust on the metal and stands in the middle of the road to goad the approaching fury, firing off a few wild shots from his pistol at the horde.

From afar, pickup truck engine running, Levi watches the situation unfold through the lenses of a pair of binoculars. The Armadillos hit the straightaway leading up to the highway and build speed as they drive under the burning trees and move through the cloud of grey smoke where the taut reaper wire slices their lives. Heads roll back from shoulders and helmets bounce along the road, spraying abstract trails of blood. Headless riders ricochet off the dirt road as the first wave skids into death and broken bikes shower the tallgrass with sparks and motorcycle parts.

Levi bends the binoculars and spots the back line of Armadillos brake in shock. A long minute of idle silence passes in the mesquite smoke haze until a bearded man dressed in all black and wearing a trucker cap climbs out of a Mack truck big rig at the back of the line with a pair of bolt cutters and clips the concertina wire. The diminished Armadillo line resumes their charge towards their prey who stands defiant a hundred yards away at the threshold of the rural highway with bright face paint beckoning like an archery target's bullseye.

Outlander turns and starts running the flat asphalt back to his pickup truck. Levi grabs his AR-15 off the seat and aims over Outlander at a lumbering red eighteen-wheeler at the back of the pack. The mysterious sheriff makes it halfway down the road to his truck when the second wave of berserkers hit the highway patrol tire shredding spikes. Motorcycles mingle and mangle at the mouth of the desolate Texas highway. A heap of carnage gathers and wipes away the threat of the gang along a rough road baking in the blaze of a mid day sun. A scattering of outlaw bikers lay wounded along the open ground in a knot of metal, miles from a hospital, as hungry vultures begin circling over the wreckage.

Outlander reaches the trucks, soaked in sweat and the haunted rodeo clown mask of paint melting in lines down his face. "Time to go. You drive while I keep watch for the eighteen wheeler." Pausing to catch his breath. "The guy driving it is called the Detroit Reaper. He's hemmed in for now but he's bad news.

A long haul trucker who hunts bikers from rival gangs. Dusts them off the road with that big rig. Repaints the cab and swaps logos for disguise." He slaps the metal on the side of Levi's truck. "We'll switch up at the state line outside of Bossier City. We need to drive all night before more cities go dark. We're in the middle of the country and the power outages are marching in from each coast. The Information Age is dying."

VICKSBURG

Day 6

Levi and Outlander arrive at the shore of a sacred Civil War battlefield at four o'clock in the morning and book passage on a riverboat named *Southern Moxie* set to head downriver into the gloom. They each pay with a one ounce numismatic gold coin from the U.S. Mint, handing it to a man named Captain Lou with a morgue cough and fingers marinating in the nicotine of a Marlboro red. Then they drive from a levee onto the lower cargo deck of a white three story boat with a black hull that sets sail on the Yazoo River heading south with its brick red tail wheel chugging and splashing through the water of a rain replenished river.

"Get some rest." Levi fishes a cold beer from a cooler in the back of his truck and hands it to Outlander. "I'll go look around and grab first watch."

Outlander sips the beer and yawns as he climbs into back of his truck to bed down while Captain Lou steers their course towards an intersect with the mighty Mississippi River.

Levi walks across the lower deck of the ship and climbs a metal staircase up to the second floor. He walks down a long musty hallway of faded burgundy carpet to a door with a white neon bar sign hanging above it, steps over a pile of vomit, and enters a small room where an all-night poker game is in progress around two circular tables holding six chairs each. A thick layer of cigarette and cigar smoke clouding the room. A pit boss bull standing watch near the window with a billy club to referee or bounce depending on the situation. The players look up from their cards and the poker chips anted onto the green felt surface. Grifters armed with .41 caliber Derringers and the gift of gab sizing him up.

"Care to take a seat, friend?" an unshaven man with bloodshot eyes asks.

"Thanks for the invite, bud, but not today. I'm just here for the whiskey." Levi nods to an old bartender with a handlebar mustache and wearing a starched red shirt that makes the man look like a mortician. "Jack Daniels, please."

The men return to their game and deal cards while the bartender pours. Levi slips the man a silver Lady Liberty coin atop a five dollar bill and asks in a low voice, "What is it that I need to know to make it back onto dry land?" The old bartender hesitates. Levi places a twenty dollar bill on the bar counter. "I don't like to drink alone. How bout you pour yourself a glass of top shelf."

The old bartender smiles, revealing yellow coffee stained teeth as he palms and slides the silver coin into his back pocket. Then pours himself a drink. "Try to stay awake. The rooms aren't safe. Too many riverboat gamblers roaming the halls." He clears his throat of phlegm, his breath carrying bad vapors that he drowns with a sip of small batch bourbon. "A gambling thirst can make a man desperate. Stand your ground but give 'em a wide berth."

"What about down below in the cargo bay?"

"Safe. They don't mess with that. That's Captain Lou's

domain. If he catches them misbehaving down there he'll toss a man overboard. Seen him do it myself a time or two. Up here, well that's fair game."

"Thank you sir."

"Safe travels young man."

Levi exits the room and returns to the lower deck as hints of a halo of dawn rise into a new day in the east. He leans on a boat rail beside his truck in the thick wet air and watches the shore as they pass by a river town where crates of cabbage and collard greens are stacked beside canvas satchels of peanuts and bales of cotton. Out in the western distance a wildfire burns on the horizon of the fertile land.

Beguiling vignettes of time flow as they sail downriver and connect with the churning current of the Mississippi. Heavy fog creeps in, obscuring the world beyond the shoreline as driftwood clangs against the hull of the boat. Superstition and angst begin to grip Levi on the voyage downriver as they sail deeper into the gloom of the Delta. Tall trees and jagged branches reach like giant thorns that blot out signs civilization as alligators slink along the surface.

An hour later, the boat sails past a spooky graveyard with tombstones leaning against the ground like crooked teeth above the mouth of the river. Mist curls on the water in the wind. A hard rain begins to fall through the brooding fog and Levi spots shapes moving in the cemetery. Feral men grave robbing the sleeping crypts for gold and jewels. The wild walk out of the fog and roll the bodies of the dead down the slope and into the river where desecrated skeletons slosh in the water and bob for a few moments, the skulls resembling bleached apples in a giant tub, before slipping below the surface and down into the deep. The hellish scene sends shivers through Levi and he grips the boat rail as floating coffins thump against the ship to haunt the voyage.

Hours downriver past the old pioneer trail of the Natchez Trace, the tendrils of mist and gloom lift. Dense forest recedes. Faint rays of sunlight glass the river as the *Southern Moxie* sails by a small town with pecan orchards, sugar mills, and old manors. The morning sun slowly burning the white fog off the meandering surface as Levi sits and dangles his legs over the swollen river and lays his arms across the boat rail, feeling the wind soothe away rough thoughts. The scenery shifts to lumber mills on shore and traffic on the river. Tugboats pushing barges upriver filled with scrap iron, timber, and coal.

Levi relaxes until a strange sight puts him on alert and on his feet. Tree sized logs from an upstream mill start moving fast past the boat, twisting in the water as they careen down river. He moves quickly to the cab of Outlander's pickup truck and lowers the tailgate. "Wake up, man. Something is going wrong on the river."

Outlander climbs out as Captain Lou sounds the horn up the bridge and steers the boat closer to shore as a buffer against the dangerous debris. They watch a barge up ahead with a tail of coal dust blowing in the wind tilt sideways into the river and lift three giant lumber poles into the air that have speared its hull. The capsizing tugboat looking like a metal bull felled by an invisible matador.

"Wait here and get ready," Outlander says. "I'm gonna talk to the captain."

"No need. River's not safe right now." A mechanic with grease stained arms and carrying a large wrench steps around the front of Levi's truck. "Lou said there's a dock two knots away that he can drop you at."

"We would appreciate that," Levi says.

The mechanic lingers. "Look, I got cleaned out last night. Need to resupply to get back into tonight's game. Help a fella out."

"We had a deal and paid good coin for passage. And we'll pay the other half once we're safe on the riverbank," Outlander says as he reaches in the front pocket of his shirt and sticks a stubby unlit cigar into his mouth. "You're welcome to a cold beer and a can of tomato juice to shake the cobwebs out. But that's all."

The mechanic's mouth locks in anger and he lunges forward, swinging the wrench hard and fast at Outlander's head. The sheriff of Shenandoah ducks under the heavy blow and catches the man on the turn, striking a vicious claw punch to windpipe with thumb tucked and four knuckles aligned. Levi winces a little as he hears something snap. The mechanic wheezes and drops the wrench, surprised eyes bulging as his grease stained palms try to lift the fatal punch from his throat. Outlander tosses the man overboard and then strikes a match on his jeans to light an ember on the tip of his cigar.

Levi watches the man float face down in the wake of the boat like gator bait.

Two knots later Captain Lou guides the *Southern Moxie* to shore just north of Baton Rouge and comes down from the bridge to see them off. Outlander drives his pickup onto the dock and waits for Levi. One at a time per their plan. Levi cranks his truck, lowers his window and rolls to a stop by Lou. He places two gold coins in the captain's hand. "Thank you for the ride. Much obliged." As Levi starts to drive onto solid ground, Lou lights a cigarette and calls after him.

"Hey, have you seen Kyle?"

"Who's Kyle?"

"The ship's mechanic," Lou says.

"He went for a swim," Levi answers.

Lou looks confused. "Kyle can't swim."

Levi drives away and follows Outlander as they vanish along a country road through veins of cypress swamps and bayous.

Later in early evening, Levi wakes from coiled nightmares

and voodoo dreams at a rest stop on the outskirts of New Orleans with the static of heat lightning popping in sticky air. He climbs out of the back of his truck and stands beside Outlander as they watch fading purple rays of the sun set in the west.

"Is it time?"

"Yes. Follow me in. If we get separated, regroup on Magazine Street across from the Vagabond River Bookstore."

They drive into the city and cross Canal Street and Tchoupitoulas, moving methodically through rain slick streets as they navigate the city grid, keeping distance from the French Quarter and Frenchman Street where people are partying to Dixieland jazz like it is the end of days. After nearly a week on the move, weary of being in any city whose lights could go out at any time, they turn onto St. Charles and keep pace alongside a green trolley car with a gold fleur de lies riding along the grass mediums of neutral ground in the Garden District. They pass by an oyster house, hot sauce shop and a shooting gallery alley where a pack of steam punks invade their arms with needles that send opiate poison into veins. They dip and pass through a neighborhood of renovated shotgun houses before turning onto the rutted roads of Magazine Street and parking in front of Dragonfly's Soda Fountain. Levi follows Outlander inside an emerald green tile walled shop that surfaces feelings of nostalgia from his childhood.

A bald old timer wearing a white button down shirt and black barkeep apron greets them from behind the counter. "How may I help you fellas?"

"Two lava chicory colas please," Outlander replies as he places a ten dollar bill on the counter and whispers. "I'm here to see Mallory."

The old man adjusts his wire rim glasses and mixes ingredients into two tall tin cups of foamy soda in silence before casually fixing light grey cataract tinted eyes on Outlander. "And who should I say is calling on her?"

"Will Dutton, sir. Her fiancé." He pauses. Unsure of the label. "I think."

"I see." The old man nods. "She thought you might be dead. Said you lead a dangerous life."

"I get that a lot, sir, but I'm very much alive. And have traveled a long way to see her."

"Wait here please," the man says as he places two bubbling glasses of lava soda on the counter and leaves the shop unattended while he goes back into the kitchen.

Levi grabs his cola and walks over to a display case filled with gourmet pastries and doughnuts shaped like little monsters. He looks over the variety while he waits. Coconut skin mummy. Licorice kiwi witch. Cherry berry goblin. Dark chocolate werewolf. Mojito rum banana hearse. House of Mirrors tapioca pudding. Risen zombie cookie dough. Maple nutmeg tangerine croissant. Pineapple coffee bean cookie. And a clever Haunted House box for to go orders.

Mallory walks through the kitchen's swinging door and catches sight of Outlander. Her black hair long and straight, highlighted with auburn streaks. She stops and breathes deep as a tear rolls out of a corner of her eye. She pushes long bangs from over her eyes with her free hand and tucks the thin hair behind an ear. Then wipes the tear away with the back of her sleeve.

"Hello darlin'." Outlander smiles shyly and feels his heart beat a little faster with happiness.

Mallory runs and leaps into his arms and they embrace. When he lets her down she leans up on her toes and kisses his cheek. Then touches the scar on his jaw. "That's new."

"We don't have much time," he says, rubbing the burned skin to shield it. "How soon can you get packed up?"

"With your help, twenty minutes," she says and points upstairs. "My apartment is on the second floor."

Levi steps outside into the humidity to give them privacy. Across the street next to a tattoo parlor, an idle poet for hire sits at a table in front of a bookstore waiting for a customer. He looks along Magazine Street with its eclectic vibe and walks down a boardwalk taking in the scene. Reading the menu on the door of a closed cafe, wishing he could have tried the Godzilla dish made of fried soft shell crab doused in remoulade sauce and speared with a knife into fried green tomatoes. Another store down he spots a newspaper stand in front of a shuttered two screen cinema, the paper inside the stand stuck on the day he flew back from Hawaii.

When Outlander and Mallory step onto the boardwalk with two suitcases, a backpack, and a box of monster doughnuts to go, Levi meets them at the trucks.

"We should drive all night," Outlander says after quickly introducing him to Mallory. "Things aren't getting any better out there."

"Fine with me," Levi says. "The closer I get to home the more anxious I get."

"While we're out there on the road you have a decision to make before we reach the Alabama line. If you want to bury your past before facing the future, detour to Apalachicola. Martial law is about to be declared. He's fair game."

They leave New Orleans on I-10, pass by an empty amusement park decaying into swampland and lit by the soft glow of moonlight, and part ways at dawn at a Highway 98 rest stop near Bayou La Batre.

"What is Secret Eden?" Levi asks as he watches tow trucks push abandoned vehicles off the road into the median to keep the flow of traffic moving.

"An EMP attack emergency plan brought forward by the solar flares," Outlander replies. "Secret Eden is a sustainability plan for surviving the crisis and the aftermath."

BOOT HILL

Day 7

Barrick Akkad stands in the parking lot of an abandoned postal depot, the asphalt sticky as it bakes in the searing sun. Drops of sweat roll down his face through beard stubble as last night's tequila sweats through his pores. Tall and slender with short blonde hair and dressed in a black shirt and khaki cargo pants, sunglasses shade his eyes as he scans the area. Across the road a vacant mall with shuttered retail stores slowly decays.

In the distance a column of black smoke rises into the sky as sirens from fire engines and police cars howl in a battle against the blaze he set in the hotel he woke up in that morning. Conveniently located on a hillside below a county jail.

Soon a staggered line of SUVs and RVs pull off the highway and loop into the facility. A passenger with unkempt hair and a thick beard hops out of the lead vehicle and jogs forward. Dressed in a tropical shirt, shorts, and sandals, Joe Rusk looks like a lost fishing boat captain. Beneath the laid back surface rests an edge primed for violence that can act with ruthless efficiency when called upon.

"Barrick," Joe says as he shakes hands.

"Rusk, glad you could make it."

"Me too, man. I was set to deploy before I got the call to join the security force at Grand Teton National Park." Joe reaches into a front pocket of his jeans and retrieves a pouch of chewing tobacco. "I wouldn't want to be stuck abroad on the Horn when the blowback begins."

"Half of our expeditionary forces are out of country," Barrick replies. "They're on their own." He glances at the stretch of vehicles. "Did you load up what you could fit from the Vegas compound?"

"Packed to the gills," Joe confirms. "And enough MREs to sustain us through the season."

"Good. Supplies are the new currency."

"We holed up outside of town yesterday waiting for you before proceeding onto the next hop."

"Got a line on the new sheriff of Great Basin National Park up the road," Barrick says. "Hoped you guys would catch up when I didn't show."

"And?"

"Basin needs a new sheriff."

Joe points to the smoke in the distance. "That your handiwork too?"

"I wanted certain resources tied up and not looking our way for the gathering." Barrick points to his pickup truck parked on the side of the depot. "Let's go. You hop in with me for the first leg. Have the men follow. We've got a long drive north into Idaho to rendezvous with the Tacoma team and the militias."

A few minutes later out on the road Joe asks, "How bad is it?"

"It's not looking good. After all these years fightin' enemies overseas, it's a complete reset. The more the lights go out, the uglier it's gonna get. Which is why we are moving north. All across the southwest, water reservoirs will run dry without electricity. Especially that giant straw poking into Lake Mead that hydrates

Vegas and Phoenix. Mayhem and looting will flow instead."

Joe shakes his head, "That will make the pension riots seem like a warm up."

"Nix sent an update from back East. NASA is saying the solar flares aren't slowing down. More are coming. This may last awhile. It's like the magnetic field around Earth is a spider whose web has been breached. The infrastructure is about to sizzle. It's unraveling, Joe. The veneer of stability is peeling back as the electrical grids go down. Few will survive the transition."

"Any large city that goes dark will turn into a stone cold kill house." Joe taps a regional map resting on the console. "Every thumb sized population center on that map is ringed by an interstate junction that will become a clogged concrete moat of instability." He spits tobacco juice into a cup and tucks a fresh pinch of chew into his cheek. "What are the viable projections?"

"Less than thirty percent of the population is projected to survive the next year in a power vacuum," Barrick answers. "We were already on the brink of scarcity before the solar storms due to planetary resource depletion and population overshoot. Ecosystems all over the world were already under strain. Insert chaos and it gets primal."

"Grim news."

"Hence our mission. My vector is the Sawtooth Wilderness." Barrick checks the rear view mirror to make sure the line of vehicles is still intact and following. "We'll hole up there for a couple of weeks to let the initial phase of the blackout burn itself out. Then we start hitting select targets to weed out challengers. Before going to ground in the vicinity of the Rockies to regroup, and repeat."

"What is the ultimate target?"

"The new capital. The federal leadership structure is locating to Defcon fallback sites around Denver and Colorado Springs. Those vanguard headquarters are now called Washington."

Joe whistles. "Quite a departure for a town that craves power above all else."

"This is all happening fast, Rusk. The government has broken apart into different factions. Congress is being regionalized. Authority is being handed down to the state level. A fragmented rearguard has been left behind in the District of Columbia," Barrick explains. "There is no consensus. Sides have been chosen. Nix and the Potomac Guard are not going to sit idle as decoys. Certain people need to be removed from the equation out West. Our mission is to eliminate and infiltrate so that the right structure is in place when the real battle begins."

"Every battle I've ever been in has felt real to me, Barrick. The whistle of a bullet has a tendency to do that."

"Not like this one. Not like the one that is coming." Barrick keeps his hand steady on the truck's steering wheel along the straight stretch of highway and glances over at his old friend. "World War III will arrive when foreign nations try to come ashore. And it will be fought in darkness. This is just the beginning. And it could take years to play out."

"It feels different this time," Joe says and shakes his head. "We're on our own soil. These are our own citizens."

"Civilization is imploding. Do you think they would feel like your fellow citizens if you were walking down the street right now in Seattle or LA with the power out?"

"No, of course not, but we've been to enough lands to know this is the best land. Is this sanctioned?

"We have the same authorization we've always had," Barrick replies. "Back channel. A layer removed. If we get caught we're nameless and faceless. No rescue, no knowledge."

Joe Rusk watches the road ahead, silent.

"This is a shadow war. And the sheriffs of Secret Eden are our first target," Barrack says as the truck speeds north along the remote road with a small private army in tow. "That is why your insert into Teton is essential. We need a mole on the inside. On the appointed day and time, we need those gates open and the guards diminished."

"Which day?" Rusk asks.

"The day you see some of these men and vehicles approaching."

Late that night deep in the frontier, a canvas of glowing stars paint the arc of the sky. And closer blinking red lights orbit against the turning Earth.

Until solar flare damaged satellites arrive dark from the other side of the world on erratic trajectories and collide. The fireworks are brief as they spread zero gravity debris. Dispersed sparkles and falling shimmers above the horizon. And then only the distant stars among the backdrop of the galaxy.

"That's space sealing us in," Joe says.

"I'll switch to CB radio from here on out and bounce messages off the bottle of the sky to maintain contact with the east team," Barrick replies as he reaches into the console and hands Rusk a wooden card. "Nix asked me to give you this."

Rusk clicks a small overhead light on in the cab and studies the carved texture along the mahogany surface. The image of a skeleton in cavalry pants and boots walking along a road, wearing a fedora with a plumed feather in the band and the brow tucked low. A bandolier belt studded with bullets wrapped over its shoulders across the bone chest plates in an X. A stubby cigar tucked into the teeth of its bone jaw.

THE
FORGOTTEN
COAST

Day 8

Levi Wolff stands barefoot on a sugar white sand beach, lean and tan, taking slow sips from a glass of fresh squeezed orange juice, his thoughts drifting with an undertow of melancholy memories of the life he had to leave behind. He stares across turquoise water as a swell of waves tumble into shore spraying salty mist into the wind, soothing the Dixie heat as a thunder storm moves over the Gulf in the distance. Then he turns and walks wet sand prints back inside a small hut as the sun dips low and melts on the horizon.

He is meeting the judge for a night cap and he wants to look presentable because in the South manners still matter. Levi enters a tiny bathroom and applies shaving cream and a razor to clear beard stubble. He looks in the mirror, his eyes a shade of sapphire blue, his face serious because his life will soon change again. In the ambient silence of the beach hut, Levi wonders if he can continue to have the strength to walk a solitary path while still holding out hope that someday he will have someone to share it with.

Evening shadows fall and the moon rises. Levi packs up his

idle Corona travel typewriter resting atop an old clementine crate and leaves the hut. He drives his pickup truck over the bridge and into the charming town of Apalachicola, stopping at the local gas station to fill the truck's tank. Paying cash and coin at the register to a fella nicknamed Bullfrog, an ex-boxer wearing denim overalls and a smiley face tie that drapes over a big belly. After exchanging vague pleasantries with the proprietor, he drives past the old Harlequin Theater. The shops along the streets buttoned up and quiet. Sea creatures safe for one more day with the local trawlers and fishing boats tucked in for the night in the port.

A restaurant nearby is hopping, serving up the day's fresh catch from hauls out in the Apalachicola River basin. Levi parks and pushes through the saloon doors of Smugglers Cove. He saddles up to the bar as a harmonica and the lazy pulls of guitar strings play in the background from a honky tonk tune.

The bartender approaches, "What can I get you started with hon'?"

He points to the taps. "A mug of the pilsner, please."

"You got it." She motions to a chalk script menu behind her. "You need time to look?"

"No, ma'am." The smell of fresh fish cooking on the grill settling it. "I'll take the grouper over mashed potatoes and a bowl of gulf gumbo to start with."

The bartender nods then lays his utensils and a bottle of Tabasco down before heading to the kitchen to relay his order to the cook.

Levi takes a long sip from the mug. Somewhere behind him a quarter slides through the jukebox and a twangy country song cuts through the silence. The gumbo arrives and he dips the spoon into the roux, staring absently into a smoke brush mirror behind a row of bourbon bottles.

The bartender returns and places his pan seared grouper

filet down on the counter. "Wanna another?" she asks pointing to his empty mug.

Levi shakes his head and digs into his meal. A few minutes later he lays his knife and fork down on the plate, and pays cash. Outside, yellow tungsten lights cast a dim glow across the empty streets of the sleepy town. He drives into the brooding night, heading away from the business district towards the residential neighborhoods as he zigzags through the square blocks. Levi passes by the Apalachicola cemetery where history rests in the shadows among heavy old tombstones below the large limbs of live oak trees dripping moss.

He continues on through the steamy night away from town until he reaches Judge Mahlon Emmett's house. Levi opens a cranky gate and climbs the steps to the porch. He checks over his shoulder, and knocks.

Mahlon answers the door with a scatter gun in hand and his jaw tense like he is chewing on a rusty nail. "Come on in."

Levi enters the foyer where a retired gavel rests atop a small stack of books on a side table in the hallway. The man's long white hair is disheveled, like he has been standing in wind. His apple colored cheeks are flush with bourbon or anticipation, perhaps a cocktail of both. Still he carries a commanding presence and dignified bearing, despite having traded in the black robed bench for a quaint nautical and Southern literature focused bookstore in the center of town.

Mahlon turns to face Levi. "Your ride is inbound." His guttural voice like a rumbling engine.

"I had hoped there would be more time," Levi says. "I like it here."

"Perhaps someday there will be. But your mission is about to begin and there is much to discuss." The judge motions his guest through the back of the house and onto a patio that overlooks the bay. "Come on back and sit a spell. I'll grab us a drink."

Levi enters a yard shrouded by wise old trees hanging moss beards from their branches. The air carrying the scent of honeysuckle vines and mimosa trees in bloom along the back fence line. He takes a seat in a rocking chair under a magnolia tree strung with globe lights.

Mahlon returns and places two glasses and a bottle of single barrel whiskey on a tree stump between the rocking chairs. Levi takes a long sip of his drink and stares out over a bluff to the dark sea. They kick up their feet and feel the wind moving from out over the ocean, into town, and down through the trees. The night grows darker and quieter. The judge leans back in his rocking chair. Levi works the cork loose on the whiskey bottle and pours another round. Something inside him acknowledges that it will be a while before he sees this mystic shore again.

"This is good stuff, Judge."

"I don't serve opossum sweat from a popskull distillery."

They sit in silence for a few minutes, sipping whiskey.

"That chessboard is different." Levi points to section of the yard where rustic three foot tall carved wooden chess pieces rest atop a board of flat stones. "Why is it full?"

"That is something I've been working on here and there in my spare time. I call it Cowboy Chess," Mahlon replies. "All eight rows and sixty four spaces occupied. Two armies per side. Traditional royal pieces toe to toe in their places along the four front rows who clash in the first wave. A light almond stain on the side of light. A dark blueberry pigment stain on the side of dark. King. Queen. Bishop. Knight. Castle. Pawn."

Mahlon rises and walks over to the board and Levi joins him. "Frontier citizens guarded in back for the final confrontation. The back row custom arranged by player freedom of choice. The pieces endowed with the same abilities. A gunslinger in place of the king. A damsel in place of a queen. A judge in place of a bishop. A bartender in place of a rook. A wild horse instead of the knight. And tumbleweed in place of pawns. Same movements. Except for the gunslinger and damsel. The gunslinger protects the damsel. The gunslinger moves all spaces and all directions. The damsel moves one space. If both the damsel and the gunslinger are captured, then it is game over."

"Why two armies facing two armies?" Levi asks.

"Because the goal is to protect the gunslinger and the damsel. When the elites clash, they keep back. The game moves fast. The mathematical possibilities endless. Subterfuge. Feints. Dodging danger as others die all around them. Then the final battle."

"I'd like to play some time when I don't have so much on my mind," Levi says.

"Oh, but you soon will, young man." Mahlon pours another round of whiskey from the bottle. "That's what it'll be like for you out there on the road when your mission begins. But on a much grander scale. And you'll be playing for keeps among the dying breed."

Levi takes a somber sip. "When do I leave?" The question seeps through the darkness.

"After you put Ivan on a slab." Mahlon pats him on the shoulder and says goodnight.

Levi falls asleep in the rocking chair, soothed into rest by the calm gulf wind, waking only once when he hears an owl hoot.

He wakes when the sun rises and he sees light come into a new day. Then he stands, puts on his grey bulletproof vest with the Secret Eden and Shenandoah patches sewn on his chest, and walks into faint morning light where he climbs into Mahlon's SUV for the thirty minute ride out to a landfill beside Tate's Hell Swamp.

"Are you prepared for what is about to happen?" Mahlon asks. "Taking a life will change your life."

"Yes. He sat on that panel in Montgomery a year ago feigning genuine interest. Shook my hand. And then dispatched a hitman to take me out that night." Levi looks Mahlon square in the eyes. "I am prepared to reintroduce myself to the man who poisoned me and upended my life."

"These people are killers," the judge warns. "They were bred for violence."

"I read the file." Levi stares out the window as the vehicle moves along a rural road away from the coast. "Ivan was a flimflam man in Tampa before the real estate crash. His slick fund almost insolvent until he became the domestic front for globalist financial mercenaries. Transnational derivative futures traders operating in a shadow world that is upending economies and bulldozing citizens. Each time their type crashes a market or starts a war, the average American citizen loses a form of freedom."

"Which idea in your presentation do you think most motivated him to try and put the zap on you?" Mahlon asks.

"Take your pick. Offshoring derivates trading to protect the financial system. Balancing the federal budget to return to a real economy with price discovery in the markets. Or protecting American sovereignty by outlawing government debt auctions to foreign lands once the amount exceeds overseas assets."

"Latest intel report indicates a yacht with underworld origins from Arkhangelsk and Warograd has set sail from Miami carrying cash and Vozroz Dust plague meth."

"They call it Mindcrawler on the west coast."

"They're supposed to rendezvous with Ivan on one of the Emerald Coast's beaches. Coast Guard cutters are trying to intercept the vessel if they can find it but there is an armada of chaos out there on the water." Mahlon turns off the road and enters the landfill. "We're here. Are you sure you're comfortable with the gears and maneuvering?" the judge asks as he lets Levi out and hands him a set of keys and photos of the guards.

"Drove a gravel truck up in Alaska for the park during paving season," Levi says. "Just got one new button to push. I'll be fine. See you back in town."

"Be on time. Two guards head to the cafe across from the Gibson Inn at seven sharp each morning to pick up bagels and pastries. The town's emergency responders have a thirty minute community meeting. It's as close to a stand down order that I could arrange. They want these guys gone before the lights go out."

Levi shrugs, "Maybe I'll return some day for one of those costume mystery weekends at the Gibson dressed as myself."

"Maybe." Mahlon extends a hand. "Good luck. After this is done, take that spur and go home and spend time with your family. Soak it up. You'll regret it if you don't."

"Right now I am focused on kicking that hornets nest." Levi looks back as he steps out into a puddle in the cool misting rain. "Don't worry. No speeches. In and out." Then he approaches a lemon skin yellow garbage truck with a burnt rust patina, climbs in, slips into blue coveralls, cranks the engine, and drives fast heading back to town.

Twenty five minutes later, a big clumsy hulk of metal rounds the corner onto Highway 98 in the middle of town, veers off the road, hops a curve, and mows over two gangsters as they sit at the Pelican Cafe under an awning sipping cappuccinos and reading the morning paper. Dying words of shocked surprise crush under the garbage truck tires as blood smears drag the sidewalk.

A crisp wind gulf wind kicks up and blows a sandwich wrapper across the street as Levi turns the wheel and aims for the alley behind Smugglers Cove where he picks up a dumpster full of last night's scraps that have simmered into hot garbage. Then drives back roads to a quiet street where a pink Panama City Beach Concrete Co. truck cuts him off at an intersection of lanes in front of a sprawling beach house that built on the combined lots of two historic cottages.

Levi slams on the brakes and presses a button on the dashboard. The garbage truck screeches tires and releases the dumpster from its jaws and the container spills rotting seafood, oyster shells, and half eaten hush puppies out onto the lawn of Ivan's estate. Diversion complete, Levi Wolff climbs out and aims to confront the concrete truck drivers.

"Hey ya dummy." A loud voice calls. "Come back here and clean this mess up." Ivan's remaining guard is out the front door and down the porch, his Bronx accent lingering like a carpetbagger. "Now man. Don't look at them. Clean it up." When the chubby man makes it to the lawn he gags and lifts his right arm, shielding his mouth with the nook of his elbow to suffocate the smell of rotting seafood, and unknowingly slowing down the response time of his distracted shooting hand.

Levi turns back to the voice, lifts his hands in surrender, and grabs a shovel from the back of the garbage truck, accidentally stepping into a fire ant hill that spreads tiny red insects with a mean bite out in a frenzy along the damp grass. Adrenaline pumping, Levi wipes his foot, barely registering the reek of the spilled dumpster as he closes distance to range. The remaining guard is hairy, with formidable muscle and strength on his frame under a layer of fat. Levi does not want to tangle with thick arms that can squeeze him like a vice. He lifts a pistol from a baggy pocket and puts shots of silenced lead in the sentry's chest until the beating heart stops. Then he drops the shovel and and continues on through a haze of gun smoke towards the target.

At that moment Ivan steps through the screen door and out onto the porch with a silk handkerchief across his mouth to block the intruding smell. Silver haired and dapper in a pale linen suit. Flashing scalding shark eyes as a thick vein rises on his forehead mainlining rage to his frontal lobe at the foul odor that seeped into his house and ruined his day. The look of a handsome idiot politician that he sported in Montgomery a year ago long gone.

Ivan starts to speak but stops as he spots his guard lying face down on his manicured lawn.

Levi aims and presses the trigger. A bullet punches a hole in Ivan's chest and his jaw falls slack as a bib of blood runs down his shirt. Levi fires one more shot in center mass as he reaches the steps.

"You?" Ivan stumbles against a porch rail making wet coughing sounds and holds up a hand. "This is you?"

Levi tucks the gun and unsheathes a blade. He cuts the air and paints a deep red line across Ivan's throat. Ivan's face flashes shock as his blood drains. Then his eyes go hollow and still. Levi grabs the body and slowly drags it down the hardwood steps to pollinate a stain of dark mystery. He drops Ivan in the driveway as the Panama City Beach Concrete Co. truck backs in.

"Geez man." A big guy with a rockabilly beard, wearing a tank top and a thick gold chain climbs down. "We were told this would be low profile."

"Not today," Levi says. "He had it coming. The lemmings are sharpening their claws."

"I'm Joey," he says with a mix of beer and sweat on his breath. His buddy riding shotgun joins him. "And that's Billy." Billy nods with a weary look, keeping his distance.

Joey takes out a hooked oyster knife and sets to work with bratwurst sized fingers. "That warrant I have up in Philly gets wiped after today. I'll be even with the law by helping send a signal that this area is under guard." He flips Ivan onto his stomach and sticks the knife under each shoulder blade and twists. "Gotta puncture the lungs to get the air out. Then run the body through the slough to break the bones and mash the rest of the air out before pouring it into a foundation. Otherwise air bubbles form."

Billy steps over and he and Joey lift Ivan up the truck ladder and tilt him into the slough. Then mash a hydraulic gear that gets the cement barrel spinning. A moment later the pink truck drives away to disappear Ivan's body in an unmarked tomb of fresh concrete at the port of Apalachicola.

Levi looks around the quiet street and notices profile faces of the neighbors peeking out from behind blinds and curtains. He ditches the garbage truck on the lawn. Unzips his stained coveralls and shrugs out of them before walking away. Wearing blue jeans, a black t-shirt covered by a grey bulletproof vest, his pecan brown cowboy boots clomping on the pavement, leaving hidden footprints of his brief time on the Forgotten Coast. Time that passed with the surfacing of pent up memory and a comet of revenge.

He weaves through the neighborhood and makes his way back to Mahlon's house where he finds a jar of Tupelo honey from Wewahatchee, referred to by the locals as Wewa, on the hood of his truck as a parting gift. Then he gets in and drives away under a patchwork of tinted clouds.

Twenty miles down the road across the bay at a terminus, Levi Wolff stands alone at the end of an empty railroad track on the outskirts of town. Pygmy palms and pine trees line the path leading north beside an aqua lagoon denting with rain rings. Thick drops of warm rain fall and fleck the white sand as churning clouds wash away the blue sky. He leans down and places a hand on the rusted steel track, feeling vibrations coursing through the rail. And waits.

Minutes later a black train rounds the bend, moving slowly as it approaches the end of the line, its forged steel wheels grinding to a halt. Levi pulls planks down from an empty flatbed car, gets in his truck, and drives up onto it. He hooks chains to the bumpers and places wooden blocks under the tires to secure his vehicle and his austere possessions inside. Then pulls the planks back into place before flashing a thumbs up signal to the conductor up ahead who blows the train's whistle in acknowledgement.

The Gulf Line train reverses direction and pulls him away, the steel zephyr building speed. He stands against the grill of his resting truck, soft rubicon rain falling, his clothes soaking in moisture and sticking to his skin, his mind knowing that the most dangerous place is the spot of ground that waits for him to arrive and die. Eventually he climbs into bed in the back of his truck and tries to sleep as the ride covers long stretches of ground up into the wiregrass region of south Alabama.

It has begun. 176,000 miles of railroad track run throughout the majesty of America. Levi Wolff is now on a warpath inside a vast maze, a seeker heading towards a dark future.

CHEAHA
WILDERNESS

Day 9

Levi wakes along the rural train ride in the early afternoon to bolts of lightning dropping like roots from the sky. He sits on the tailgate of his truck in thick energized air watching good pastureland and red clay roads sweeping by. Catching the subtle scent of a strawberry patch before passing by a field of wild radishes. The tracts of land stream by and change to rows of tall leaf Choctaw tobacco flanking the sides of the tracks before morphing into a wide span of white tipped blooming cotton. Then the scenery shifts to farmers on earth chewing combines threshing maize and harvesting peanuts and soybeans. Images in motion taking him through small towns plowed by neglect due to idle factories aging with quiet dignity, populated by resilient country folk flying the American flag from their front porches. Landmarks testifying that hard times arrived long before the Aurora Terra.

The train enters a small village in Talladega county along an old Indian trading route and stops across from a sunflower farm at the Grumpy Grist Mill where a wooden wheel turns in a thin river to nourish energy back through to the heavy stones inside grinding grain crops to flour. While the train loads supplies, Levi hops down and relaxes when he hears the familiar honey drawl of the women and the languid accents of the men. He pays cash for a plate of hickory smoked brick pit beef BBQ over yellow corn grits that he eats down by the stream next to a copper moonshine distillery until the train whistle blows.

The train conductor who is pushing seventy years of age meets him at the flatcar to help him unload his truck. "I'm Nelson."

"Levi." They shake hands.

"I'm gonna head up the track just yonder the speedway." Nelson takes out a handkerchief and wipes sweat pooling in the etched age lines of his weathered face. "You got four hours. Ain't much but that is all I can spare. Gotta schedule to keep. And a granddaughter waiting on me for supper when I finish this run. Is that enough time for you to do what you gotta do?"

"It'll have to do, sir." Levi stares up a country road leading from the grist mill through tall pines trees to a sign at the edge of the Talladega National Forest. "Please tell Mahlon thank you for me. Didn't get the chance to say goodbye."

"I'll tell that rascal on Sunday morning at church." Nelson lifts his cap so that the bill pushes a shadow over his eyes. "You know the judge can't carry a hymn without making a baby cry? I'm not kiddin'. Has whiskey stained vocal chords that can split glass. But he's rock solid and I'm proud to call him my friend."

Levi laughs and it feels good to let some stress release with it. "Thank you for the first leg of the ride, sir." He pulls a map from his pocket marked with directions to the homestead that Mahlon drew for him. "Well, I should get to it."

"See you down the road." Nelson walks back up the line of tracks.

Levi rolls the truck windows down and drives away into a dense green forest of pine scented air, weaving his way towards his family's hidden homestead. A half hour later he parks at the end of a mulch driveway and walks through wild grass glazed with dewdrops and dotted with large stretched loblolly pine cones. He steps onto a porch lined with rocking chairs and knocks on the door.

For a few hours, precious time passes like a dream and the problems roaming the world outside dissipate. His worries about being away from his immediate family during a time of civilization shifting turmoil ease a bit with peace of mind when he sees firsthand how his family traded city life for cozy frontier life. The homestead having been stocked with a year's worth of supplies. Food, water, medicine, batteries, matches, books, tools, guns, and ammunition.

When Levi spots an empty bunk waiting on him to return home someday, he knows that at night out on the road he will dream about this homestead. An aching melancholy tugs at his heart when dusk arrives and the flicker of lightning bugs glows in the woods as he says goodbye after such a short visit, knowing that perhaps he will not survive long enough to return.

He links back up with Nelson's train on the north end of the county beside the speedway. A new conductor hops aboard and the ride arcs up alongside the Birmingham skyline, moving past the Magic City's iron ore scrapyards, medical facilities, and lush urban parks. Drops of rain fall on the windshield of the strapped down pickup truck. Levi leaves Alabama behind for an unknown amount of time as the train travels along the Nickajack route, passing into Tennessee and through Chattanooga and Chickamauga.

By the time the train reaches Bristol, his hand crank radio reports new solar flares and geomagnetic storms striking the atmosphere and taking down the electricity grids in Southern Europe and parts of South America. As Levi listens to NASA scientists on the radio warning more are coming, he thinks back to pioneer America, pre-electricity. A time when the space weather phenomenon of the Aurora Terra would have provided spectacular nocturnal ribbons of color in the Equatorial night sky without disrupting civilization.

Then a doctor from the CDC on the AM radio panel challenges that view when he comments that all six historically recorded global superflu pandemics, the most recent being after World War I, coincided with a year of maximum solar activity.

SHENANDOAH

Day 10

Levi exits Interstate 66 a few hours southwest from the capital and drives along a back road leading to three hundred square miles of wilderness. The surrounding countryside starts to lighten by the time he rolls to a stop in front of a barrier along a quiet road with colonial snake fence zigzagging stacked beams of timber through thick grass. He reaches for the dashboard radio and turns down the volume on an Appalachian tune with a violin and guitar dueling.

A young National Guard soldier with straight red hair and freckles approaches his window, her serious eyes scanning the Secret Eden and Shenandoah patches on his grey vest. "Name?"

"Levi Wolff."

The soldier flips through sheets on a clipboard and makes a checkmark. "You will need to pass through an inspection at the old visitor center below camp before heading up to Skyland Lodge." She hands over a park pamphlet and then motions to a member of her squad to lift the gate.

Levi drives across the southern boundary of Shenandoah National Park and climbs the incline of Skyline Drive. Miles of silence spin into the odometer as he curves past guardrails of stacked stone and scenic overlooks obscured by thick fog. For the next hour he follows the yellow line of the meandering mountain road within a bubble of limited visibility. Eventually reaching Skyland.

He parks inside an oval meadow atop the mountain. The half mile radius split by a road that cuts across the Appalachian Trail. On the empty right side, wild varieties of colonial bent, deertongue, poverty oat, low panic, and orchard grass grow tall. Complimented by colorful butterflies dancing across the stems and buzzing marble sized bees whipping about in the fresh air, while off near the tree line, a doe and her two fawn graze on dew drop grass as smoky fog creeps across the Virginia meadow, shrouding miles of valley visibility.

On the left side of Skyline Drive, a hill rises up to a mountain peak dotted with granite boulders inside a perimeter of log cabins. A thin ribbon of pavement connecting the visitor center complex below to the lodge above. Levi parks his truck in front of the forty yard long, single story converted visitor center complex set parallel to the main road. A wall of reflective windows blending the rectangular limestone structure into the natural surroundings as camouflage.

He gets out of his truck and stretches his legs after the long drive from Bristol. The temperature is mild and the cool air scented with burning maple logs from a short chimney jutting up through the roof beside an igloo sand bag nest for sentries to guard the approach from high ground. Levi walks into the lobby of the visitor center, cowboy boots clomping of the floorboards.

Outlander is at the fireplace stirring a metal pot hanging above glowing coals. He looks up and smiles. "You made it, man. Welcome to Shenandoah." They shake hands. "Coffee?"

"Please."

Outlander grabs a mug from the mantle, scoops it into the

pot, and passes the steaming cup to Levi. "Give me a sec and then I'll show you around." The sheriff grabs a log from a stack of chord wood and places it in the fireplace. Then takes an old newspaper, twisting the paper in his hands until it forms a torch of knotted words, and strikes a match to light the pages, waving them under the bark until smoke begins to rise from the wood. The fire grows as the faint blue tips of the yellow flames burrow into the logs. "Got a lot of people coming through the gate today. Most won't stay long and will move along. One of my job duties is to screen everyone before they enter to make sure they don't pose a security risk."

Levi takes a sip of coffee and nods.

"There are three sections of the visitor center," Outlander continues. "Barracks on the north end for a platoon of soldiers. A gym in the middle," he says pointing through a glass wall at barbell free weights, benches, exercise stations, climbing ropes dangling from the ceiling like dried twisted snakes, punching bags, kickboxing equipment, and mock weapons stacked in the corners. "We will be training with Mallory at daylight each day before breakfast. Don't let her wiry petite frame fool you," Outlander warns Levi. "She's got honed skills."

"I only met her for a second in New Orleans. What's her story?"

"She moved around a lot as a kid. A military brat. Her mom is native Alaskan Inupiat. Her dad a Texan. She was a chef for a cruise line." Outlander refills his cup of coffee from the pot of strong brew in the fireplace. "That's how we met. I was on vacation detoxing from a tough assignment and we hit it off an excursion tour in Italy. Ended up keeping in touch. I'd go undercover and she'd go to sea on six month stints." Outlander steers Levi out of the lobby to the library on the south side of the visitor center. "Anyway, for Mallory, practicing self defense helped her combat the claustrophobia of the ship and ensured that she could defend herself in tight quarters against crew or passenger."

"So how long had it been since you'd seen one another?" Levi asks.

"Eight months. A long time. We hadn't spoken in two." Outlander scratches the scar on his jaw and sighs. "Long story. Complicated. Still haven't talked it out or worked through it yet. Soon though." He clasps Levi on the shoulder. "Enough of that. Now back to the matter at hand."

Levi points to a map of America tacked to the library's east wall. "Is that what I think it is?"

"Those push pins show growing areas without electricity. Dead zones," Outlander nods gravely. "The cities hold millions. The countryside thousands. The wilderness path we're on is specifically designed to avoid population density and therefore will involve hundreds."

Levi sits on a table and stares out over the meadow while he sips his coffee. "So how many of us are there here?"

"One hundred max at any time," the sheriff answers. "A platoon of sixteen soldiers. Less than ten fixed operatives who will stay in a short row of cabins split off from the lodge. Each with their own missions. The rest transient and temporary." Outlander points over Levi's shoulder. "See that grove of rhododendron shrubs just behind where you parked your truck? Tomorrow we're going to establish an outdoor firing range to sharpen shooting skills. Target practice will take place daily after breakfast. That'll leave you late morning and afternoons for your work. Wanted to do it today but a crew is busy barricading and sealing the north gate and side entrances. The capital is in a frenzy. People hustling about in secrecy. Too risky to leave 'em open."

Levi lifts his cup to finish his coffee but his left hand starts shaking slightly so he places the cup on the table and stands, pacing to calm his nerves.

The sheriff of Shenandoah fastens his eyes on Levi. "Now, how was your mission?"

"Cleansing."

"And?"

"Brutal. I haven't slept much since." Levi hesitates, realizing that Outlander had given him the lay of the land while also sizing up the aftershocks of his detour along the Forgotten Coast. "Racing thoughts. Hard to slow 'em down." Levi pushes his hands into his pockets and shrugs. "Vivid dreams too."

"Take the day off. You're not ready to get started yet." A look of concern on his face. "Go clear your head. Get your mind right. A thunderstorm swept through the area overnight. There's a damaged campsite that needs to be rebuilt so that it can serve as a lookout nest." Outlander lifts a park pamphlet from a table beside him and unfolds it. He points to a spot on the map. "Right there. Leave your truck and stuff where you're parked. Hike down to it and camp there for the night. The weather will be clear."

Levi starts to counter but is interrupted.

"That's an order. Not an option." Outlander heads back out to the lobby and grabs his khaki canvas satchel. He reaches in and hands Levi a key. "Cabin 7. You can start moving your things in tomorrow. You'll be working alongside someone from the Smithsonian archive. Her name is Naomi. She's inventorying the boxes now up the hill. The last batch is supposed to arrive this afternoon. Once you catalogue the numbers you need, the documents can be shredded down here in a room off the library. The paper and ink are chemical free and environmentally friendly so the shreds can be composted. No trace."

Levi nods and exits the lobby in silence. Out on the sidewalk a man the size of a bodybuilder with long black hair and streaks of grey blending in walks past and bumps shoulders with him. Levi glances back.

He turns and catches Levi's stare. A thin line of discoloration traces a wavy line across his forehead as if a strand of hair fell away and burned a pale scar into the skin. "Pardon me. Tired is all. Long drive in." An unreadable face and big white chomper teeth smiling before walking into the building.

Outlander watches the exchange with narrow eyes. The man approaches while Levi rummages around in the back of his truck under the hardtop changing into hiking shoes and gathering a pack and supplies from the long boxes that horseshoe around his bunk.

"Morning, sheriff. I'm Clay Donegal." He fishes identification out of a front pocket of his red and black checked flannel shirt. "Passing through and heard this might be a safe place to stop and rest for the night before traveling on."

"State Department, huh." Outlander studies the ID while trying to get a measure of the man. "You don't look like State."

"I was in security." Clay's voice deep and as strong as his frame. "Not the diplomatic corp. Worked some overseas alphabet soup along the way too."

Outlander glances outside at the overcast sky and watches Levi cross the road into the tall grass of the meadow and vanish into the fog as unmarked government SUVs arrive carrying other operatives. "Where ya heading?"

"Offutt, Nebraska to retrieve my change of station orders from a vault. Flight in was diverted to Baltimore. Trying to make my way over."

Outlander pauses, stalling for a decision of intuition, sensing deception. "There's a rest stop seventy miles down the road at the West Virginia line. It's safe and well lit."

"That's not much of a welcome home after two years abroad." Clay shakes his head with disappointment.

"Well that's the way of the road." He hands the identification back. "Can't let you pass."

"All right then." The man pockets his ID and turns to walk away, glancing back once to nod a goodbye.

Outlander could tell the stranger wanted to say more.

Beyond the tree line outside, Levi Wolff hikes along the Appalachian Trail, navigating south. The sea of green vegetation that he had grown accustomed to in the spring and summer fading away in the changing seasons, creating early autumn fields where golden stalks blend with tints of cinnamon. Mixing with evergreen trees and foliage as his movement carries him deeper into the wild. Complex thoughts drop along the soggy forest trail in the Blue Ridge Mountains. He walks with a full pack of gear hanging on his back as stress and anxiety are temporarily discarded cargo. Mud clings to his hiking shoes, masking the lava shards wedged in the tread of the soles. A few more miles of rough hiking and stream crossings will shed the final traces of his Pacific summer.

When the path intersects with the Mill Throng trailhead, Levi turns left into woods sloping under the cloud line and begins his descent alongside a replenished mountain stream spilling with recent rain. The water moves with a soothing hum that drowns out distracting thoughts and ushers Levi deeper into nature unbound. Nourished roots from ancient trees ripple the ground. Granite rocks in varying sizes hunker in the stream and form a skeleton for the flow. He pauses briefly to perch on the edge of a moss rock a few inches above the stream, dips his canteen into the cold water and waits for the liquid to trickle through a charcoal filter embedded in the nozzle. Then he takes a long sip that soothes his dry throat.

Further downhill, the stream washes out the trail. Brown earthy puddles lap at his shins as he steps into them. Fallen trees poke across the path in staggered intervals, culled by the thunderstorm. A diverse array of still standing trees shed into the wind as leaves slowly die their way through the fall season. As he walks, Levi tries to time the motion of the falling leaves as they twist towards his outstretched fingers. Browns, yellows, reds.

Autumn flakes that bend away.

Levi checks his map, navigates over debris and downhill another mile until reaching a flooded primitive campsite above Rapidan camp. After surveying the area, he decides to move the site uphill to drier ground on a small knob in the trail. He notes the change on his map with an *X* and inks an *O* to mark the submerged spot. Then he slips knee length waders over his shoes and plunges into a clogged portion of the stream. The current pushes against Levi and keeps him off balance until he adjusts his footing and grows accustomed to the shifting rush of water as he begins to lift cabbage sized rocks from the stream bed and place them up on the trail.

When a rock mound finally forms, Levi hops out, removes the waders and takes a break. All around him, hidden birds sing from the balcony of high branches, their throats working like flutes. Songs from the scarlet tanager, indigo bunting, cedar waxwing and cerulean warbler spreading a calmness across the mountain as thin mist cools the beads of sweat dripping down his face. He acknowledges a growing appetite and removes dried figs, shelled pecans and beef jerky from the top pouch of his pack, chewing the flavors slowly while enjoying the freedom of being alone in the woods. Washing it down with the last can of sarsaparilla cola he bought at the rest stop vending machine in Arizona.

Levi looks out in the distance to rolling hills where the tops of trees rise above hollows full of fog on the threshold of Shenandoah Valley. Fall foliage with rusted and golden colors run along the hills. He resumes his work and hauls the stones up to the new campsite. Placing each one along a curving rim until a boundary forms. Then Levi returns to his pack and removes a folding shovel, ax and hatchet, leaving the plastic encased chainsaw idle. He sheds his jacket and begins digging a concave pit inside the rock ring, pushing down into dirt and clay. The harder he works through the hours of silence, the stiller his mind becomes. A coexistence of exertion and inner rest forms. Taking deep breaths of mountain air that places a mild wood taste on his tongue. He is exactly where he is supposed to be at this moment. Relaxed even while in motion.

By late afternoon, a thick Appalachian fog hangs in the cold air as a light rain trickles through the trees. Levi finishes spiking the corners of his tent shelter and moves to his pack. Fingers stained with dirt work to unfasten the rope around the tarp. He frees the bundle and carries it over to the campsite. Then he unrolls the canvas until dry cords of chopped wood appear along with smaller ties of twigs and sticks. He stacks the largest pieces into the center of the pit and the tops them off with the twigs and a handful of damp pine needles. Medium sized sticks are poked into the crevices of the logs so that the strands can carry the fire down to the base. The last step places the tarp over the pyramid to keep the wood dry until the sun sets.

Then the forest changes with the rustling sound of movement upon fallen leaves. A beautiful woman with sun kissed skin and sandy blonde hair pulled up in a ponytail, wearing blue jeans and a pale yellow rainproof pullover, rounds the bend of the trail. "Hi. Are you Levi?" she asks, her voice carrying the trace of a western accent as her smoldering jade eyes study him.

"Yes," Levi says, wiping dirt and sweat from his brow. He notices a small purple wildflower tucked behind her ear.

"I'm Naomi," she blushes as they shake hands. "Outlander said it would be okay to hike down here to meet you. The rest of the boxes of files should arrive later today. Did he tell you that I'm with the Smithsonian archives?"

"Yes, he said we would be working together."

"There isn't much time, Levi." She takes a seat on a freshly cut log stump across from him in the ring of the campsite. "Freshwater and food are being rationed below the mountain and beyond the valley. We need to talk and operate with a sense of urgency if this is going to work."

"Okay."

"Part of my role at the Smithsonian as a historian was to catalog confidential archives. Including data on the true state of America's debt fueled economy. Not the fluff that gets pushed in the press. The boxes up at the lodge in your cabin and two doors down in mine have the full data, not the mirage."

"What kind of secret archives?" Levi stares into her green eyes and notices flecks of copper tint in the iris.

"Are you familiar with the Manassas Plan?" Naomi asks.

"No."

"One of the first battles of the War Between the States occurred just up the road. After the Confederates routed the Union forces, they could have marched all the way to the capital and seized the city." She stands and walks to the edge of the flowing creek and stands next to a moss covered rock. "When World War I broke out and began pulling America towards Europe, the Battle of Manassas served as a lesson to the War Department. The Federal Reserve was created in the spirit of the original thirteen colonies to serve as a backup capital plan. Twelve branches and the Denver Mint spread out across the land in case the capital was captured by an enemy army. With no single city inheriting capital power. A dispersed republic instead." Naomi takes a sip of water from her canteen before continuing. "There is already a clash occurring in the capital along intellectual bloodlines. A dangerous power struggle between the District of Columbia and the Defcon Denver fallback plan."

Levi holds up a hand. "I need time to process that."

Naomi folds her arms across her chest. "Why did you write the paradigm?"

"Because the economy seemed fake, like an optical illusion. Financial engineering masking the reality. Congress unable to help the situation, only hurt it. I tried to construct a model that would help pick up the pieces one day when the system implodes."

"Go on," Naomi encourages. "It's a blueprint isn't it?"

"Yes. Trillions of dollars printed out of thin air from where? Backed by what? Ninety percent of money is electronic. We're here now because digital ones and zeroes are dying in the darkness." Levi goes to his backpack and unzips a side pocket. He hands Naomi two folded pages. "It's the latest version. We will need to attach a lot of data and numbers to it."

Naomi puffs wet bangs out of her eyes. "So we begin tomorrow?"

"Yes.

Naomi smiles and winks at him. "See you tomorrow, Levi." She adjusts the wildflower tucked behind her ear and walks away, fading into the dusk at the bend of the trail.

The sound of the rushing stream and drizzle of rain nourishing the mountain helps him think. After a few minutes, he grabs the chainsaw beside his rucksack and carries it downhill to an American chestnut tree laying on its side across the trail. He yanks the ripcord on the chainsaw's tail in a quick, hard motion and the tranquility shatters as an electric buzz roars through the forest, scattering the birds. Then he places the blade against the trunk's bark and digs into wooden skin that bleeds sawdust.

When night falls over the forest, Levi Wolff rests on a stump in solitude beside the warm glow of the campfire, savoring the nocturnal sounds of Shenandoah, a national park whose name was bestowed by the Iroquois, a name that means "daughter of the stars."

LIBERTY
DOLLAR MAP

<u>ONE</u>
Establish 12 new Congressional seats reserved for American Indians. 2 Senators and 10 Representatives from the Cherokee, Choctaw, Seminole, Mohawk, Blackfeet, Apache, Comanche, Sioux, Lakota, Hopi, Navajo and Athabascan area nations.

<u>TWO</u>
Monetize the environment in order to protect it. Establish recycling depots for stockpiling infrastructure materials in populated counties. Transform the U.S. Postal Service into the U.S. Postal & Recycling Service.

<u>THREE</u>
Create a National Service Corp to help weather unemployment with infrastructure projects that benefit all. Redirect idle resources. Tear down abandoned buildings, salvage their materials, and reclaim the land as wild. Broker and ship extra raw materials, metals, and food overseas to pay down foreign debts using the Merchant Marine fleet.

<u>FOUR</u>
Outlaw auctions of American sovereignty that sell government debt to foreign nations. Pivot from being a perpetual debtor nation and into a sustainable economy. Balance the federal budget to see the real economy. Reduce federal government spending by 5% per year until deficits end. Limit interest rates for any lending to 10% or less. Send derivatives speculation and futures trading offshore to quarantine America. The economy does not have to be a riddle. It can transform into a model of dynamic simplicity to help repair America.

<u>FIVE</u>
Take all previous individual annual payments into the Social Security system and convert them into 30-year treasury bonds with 2% interest accrual factored in so that they can be redeemed throughout life.

<u>SIX</u>

Convert American fiat currency into a tangible and
sustainable currency that helps society. Finance
projects by converting liabilities into assets and
fund them with the monetary swing.

(A) Liabilities: Subtract national debt, state
debt, local debt, collective private debt, acres of
polluted land and water, unemployed citizens, and the
number of incarcerated citizens.

(B) Assets: Add land area divided into natural,
industrialized, commercial, and residential
categories. Fossil fuel reserves. Alternative energy
output. Hectares of cultivated land. Agricultural
yield. Clean freshwater supply. Miles of navigable
coastal land. Health of fishing stocks in territorial
waters. Pounds of precious metals. Levels of
stockpiled metals. Trade skill and education levels.
Historical and cultural assets of museums and parks.
Patents, trademarks and copyrights. Health of
indigenous species. Military resources. Roads and
bridges. Transportation vehicles. Private property
and privately held assets. Expand the gross domestic
product list once the foundation stones are in place.

(C) Formula: Assets minus Liabilities equals
American Equity.

<u>SEVEN</u>

Establish five currency color categories. Printed
greenbacks for tangible assets. Bluebacks to reflect
international trade velocity of goods in transit. Red
for default and future barter repayments. Orange for
sunsetting unsustainable unfunded liabilities unless
an 8th continent is discovered on Earth. Purple
tinted currency for the monetary swing created by
infrastructure and environmental protection projects
that turn liabilities into assets.

SHENANDOAH

Day 11

Levi unlocks his pickup truck at the visitor center and drives uphill to the lodge where he dips off the road and parks in a clearing beside Cabin 7. His cabin sits at the end of a row connected to Skyland's stone main lodge. He hauls some gear to the cabin and sets his bags down on the steps, glancing around at the secluded offshoot. The section just far enough away from the bulk of the cabins across the way to be private and partially hidden from view.

He pulls back the screen door and inserts the key into the lock. Levi enters a minimalist room with wood panel walls and a floor stacked with cardboard boxes. The furniture sparse and efficient with a bed, end table, rocking chair and desk set beneath a bay window. Levi drops his bags in a walk in closet at the back left corner of the room just beyond a small bathroom.

Back outside he walks a cobbled path to Skyland Lodge and enters the lobby where framed black and white photographs hang along the rustic walls. An alcove holds a vacant check in counter and a thin staircase leading up to a second floor room. A cozy den waits with plush sofas and a wall of windows that face out over the grey hidden valley. Empty rocking chairs line a porch that until recently had tourists relaxing during the lengthy intermission between sunrise and sunset. He peeks into an adjoining dining room with maroon carpet and thick rafters dangling wrought iron chandeliers over empty tables. Then takes a spiral staircase that descends to the tavern. The low ceiling, dark lighting and antique bar gives the feel of stepping back in time. Levi lingers for a moment before heading back upstairs.

On his way back to his cabin he stops when the door to Cabin 2 opens and a tanned bald man wearing blue dungarees and a white shirt steps out with a toolbox in hand.

"Hey. I'm Bart," he says in a raspy voice that Levi at first mistakes for laryngitis as they shake hands.

"Levi. Good to meet you."

"Which one is yours?" Bart asks.

"Seven," Levi replies. "Do you know who else is on the row?"

"Mallory is in 3," Bart says. "Jody in 4. But we won't be seeing much of her. She's doing field work in the area inspecting TVA hydroelectric dams. Naomi in 5. Outlander is in Cabin 1 above the alcove in the lobby. A medic will be in 6." Bart points across the way at six larger cabin units dispersed across the mountain top in a log hewn half moon. "Those are called Piedmont, Blackrock, Hawksbill, Lynchburg, Blacksburg, and Doubletop. That's where the transient government workers will stay."

"I imagine Outlander wants us to keep our distance," Levi says as he watches a hawk soar above, catch an updraft in its wings, and hover scanning for prey.

"Yup. Conversation vague and light," Bart explains, his voice hoarse. "We'll probably only see them at meal time. They'll mostly be resting for trips to other lily pads."

"Where did you arrive from?" Levi asks as three arriving crows squawk and chase off the hawk which dips over the tree line and descends into the valley.

"The Department of Agriculture's sugarcane biofuel research division on the Gulf Coast," Bart says. "Each park gets a mechanic."

"That's good to hear," Levi says pointing towards his truck. "Everything that I own is in there. I've got supplies to barter with if you wouldn't mind checking her over when you get time."

"That's a deal. My jeep is parked down at the visitor center," Bart says. "About to go fiddle under the hood. See you at dinner?"

"See you then. I'm gonna go get settled in." Levi enters his cabin and forgoes unpacking. He is used to living out of a backpack. He walks to the closet and withdraws a small cylinder of brushed steel wrapped in a velvet cloth from a side pocket of his hiking pack. The tube contains a tiny parchment rolled into a scroll. Custom calls for the *mezuzah* to be affixed to the doorpost of a dwelling, but Levi decides not to. This room is temporary. It is not home. Levi carries home in his heart. It has been like this for a while. He places the *mezuzah* on the end table beside the bed and leaves his cabin.

He connects with a trail down the hill and hikes for some exercise, stopping every so often to take in the view along a spot of the 101 miles of the Appalachian National Scenic Trail within the park. Later in the day while passing by a mile marker, he remembers that the original pathway from Georgia to Maine, before Alabama's Pinhoti Trail was linked, covered 2160 total miles, the same number as the length of time in a Zodiac age, and the same number as the diameter of the moon. Levi pushes the thought away and moves deeper into the woods, not returning to his cabin until late in the afternoon for a long nap.

That night, a few cabins away, Outlander knocks on Mallory's door and hears soft jazz music playing through the windows. He catches his reflection and starts to smooth his hair back and brush it into place with his fingers. The door opens and he drops his hands to his side, then stuffs them into his pockets.

"Wanna take a walk with me?"

"You look tired. We're just getting started here." Her hazelnut eyes looking him up and down. "You need to get some sleep and take better care of yourself."

"I know." Outlander shrugs and smiles sadly. "It's just that memories are surfacing. Ones I've been doin' alright keeping down until now."

Mallory steps out on the porch, shutting the door behind her, and scoots up on the porch railing, kicking her legs in the cool night air. "You were gone a long time."

"I know." Outlander rests his forearms on the rail and stares off into the night. "Many times."

"And you always came back different."

"Too much lost time. I shoulda quit long ago and joined some small police force in a nice place." He pushes off the rail and starts to pace. "I feel a lot of guilt when I look at you."

"Is that all you see when you look at me?" she asks and holds her eyes on him.

"No." He makes brief eye contact. "I also see someone that I'd like another shot at having a life with."

Mallory nods once in acceptance of his honesty. She glances out over the mountain top, the features of her youthful face bunching together slightly while she thinks. Then she swings her legs back over the rail and hops down onto the porch. "Let's take that walk." Mallory smiles at him. "You don't have to get all gussied up for me," she says pointing to her jeans and sweatshirt as she puts on a cap. "I'm just concerned that you look worn out."

They head down to the meadow and intersect with Skyline Drive as fog rolls over the mountain and masks the dark road. After a mile of heading due south they stop at a little shack with a long roadblock pole lowered and locked into place. Outlander takes out a key and unlocks the hut door. They enter a cramped room and set their pistols down on a ledge.

"No lights." Outlander unzips a flap on his backpack and takes a seat on a stool in front of a window facing the road. He dips into his pack and removes a bottle of red wine and a Swiss Army knife. While he works on the cork, she pulls out the other stool and takes a seat next to him. "I got that bottle in California the day I found out I'd be heading here. I thought it would help us unseal our memories. Say what has to be said. And move on together." He pops the cork and passes the bottle to Mallory.

She sets it down on the ledge. "It needs a little time for the air to wake it up."

Their knees touch as they stare out into the night. The yellow reflectors on the road ebbing in and out of the fog.

"You're the reason I'm here," she says. "I wouldn't have come if I didn't think there was a chance we could repair the distance between us."

"I can't do this and worry about you somewhere out there," he says softly. "We need to be beside each other. Whatever is coming in the darkness. Whatever happens."

"You never told me the whole story. I wanna hear it. We're in total isolation. Solar flares popping every few days and wiping large swaths of nations into total darkness. The details can't endanger me now. A different danger has arrived." She takes a gulp of wine and hands the bottle to Outlander. "I like it here. It's quiet except for the sounds of nature and I find those soothing."

Outlander takes a long sip from the bottle. "Are you still my fiancée?"

"We're not nearly there yet, Will. If and when I am truly ready you won't have to ask. It'll just happen naturally. Now tell me what happened," she pushes a tear to a corner in her eye. "Please."

"Ally, I tried to save him." The memory floats around the small shack. "I just couldn't get to him in time. It all went down quick. And I was too far away."

"I know you did," she says as she squeezes his arm. "You were Brad's best friend. It goes without saying."

"One night in Laredo we'd had a few too many beers. The Porter Draw persona surfaced. His eyes grew cold and he told me he had to pop two Valium to sleep through the night. That the deep cover work was draining his battery." Outlander shakes his head. "That scared me bad because he was the toughest man I ever met. Hands down. Guns on the table. And the best lawman I ever served with. What did that mean for me?" He shakes his head. "Now I know."

They fall silent in the guard hut, watching the night and subtle bends in light and motion. Mallory and Outlander share another sip of wine and then he slips his hand into hers. "I still remember what he said to me that night in Yuma when we were knocking back shots of tequila after getting our orders." Mallory leans her head down on his shoulder. Outlander's eyes harden. "He said he'd lived in the shadows of America's mean streets and transient ports for far too long. That he was done after we finished infiltrating the Armadillos. Planned on heading back to his family's lake house in Duluth and working at a hardware store."

"How did he die?" she asks.

"Hard. But quick. We had seen a lot. I was in Tucson at the time. He was outside of Reno on a run, camping out in the desert with some guys. Had a bad dream and called out in his sleep. The Armadillos said it sounded like cop speak. They never said what he said but it spooked them. That was that. They made a phone call. Then they shot him in his sleep and rode away, leaving him there on open ground."

"So that's why you stopped speaking to me?"

"I was in a dark place. Knew they suspected me too because we patched in together. Didn't know for sure though. Couldn't take that risk. Needed you far away and safe." He looks over at her. "A month ago I snatched three on a borderland buy along the Salton Sea. Tossed the first one down an abandoned mine shaft. Then the remaining two told me I wasn't compromised. That the Armadillos didn't know for certain. Just suspected. I believed them."

"Are they still out there?" Mallory asks.

"I doubt it. I shot the second one to see if the third's story would hold. It did. I took the keys to his bike and left the third man there in the desert unarmed. And drove off. Last time I looked back he was being chased by a pack of wild coyotes."

"I read the papers afterwards," she says. "Seven members of that gang mysteriously died two days after Brad was killed. By the time they found his body, a biker war had started in Washington state that spread halfway up the Alcan and straight down Highway 1." Mallory pauses. "How did you create such a chain reaction?"

Outlander says nothing as he tips the wine to Mallory. "Last sip." She shakes her head and he drains the final few ounces before setting the bottle down on the ledge. "I heard a rumor at an old saloon outside of El Paso," he says, "that some guy broke into their clubhouse, stole their guns, drugs, cash, and the spare keys to their bikes. Then he dropped all that stuff off across town on the doorsteps of their rivals. Apparently when word got around they went to go get their contraband back. That didn't go so well."

"Apparently," she replies with a touch of amused sarcasm. "And what about the riot at Pelican Bay that took out the gang leaders that approved the hit on Brad?"

Outlander shrugs, "Maybe the stolen goods were used as a down payment on a reverse prison hit using the Armadillos' own ill-gotten gains."

"And then you get exiled?" she asks as she grips his hand.

"Something like that. Exile and a slew of threats that I'm still under investigation," he says in a low growl as he turns his head and brushes Mallory's bangs away from her cheek, their faces just a few inches apart. "I hit their Texas chapter a few days ago while Levi and I were making our way cross country." He leans closer and gently presses his thumb on her lower lip. Mallory nods ever so slightly as Outlander's other hand grazes the goose bumps on her neck as he reaches up and slips off her cap. The tips of Mallory's raven black hair fall to her shoulders as they kiss.

She pulls away. "How long can we stay here like this?"

"We don't have to be back until dawn."

Mallory reaches into a small pocket in her jeans and takes out her engagement ring, a fire behind her eyes. "Every girl likes to feel special and pretty," she says as she slips his ring back on her finger.

SHENANDOAH

Day 12

After spending the afternoon processing boxes of agricultural and oceanic data, Levi and Naomi's eyes grow tired and their bodies restless.

"Wanna take a break and grab some exercise?" she suggests while stretching and covering a yawn with her hand.

"Yeah, I'd like that. I need a change of scenery. I'm losing focus."

On the walk down to the visitor center Naomi seems distracted.

"Headache?" Levi asks as they enter the gym.

"No, just thinking. Why did you list American Indian Congressional seats as the first aspect of the Liberty Dollar Map?" Naomi asks as she climbs on an exercise bike and begins pedaling.

"Because we left the indigenous American Indian values behind that we will need to navigate the future," Levi says as he racks free weights and begins reps on bench press. "America's population has grown tremendously over the past two hundred plus years. Adding twelve native seats is doable. It would help the Constitution spread deeper roots."

"I just hope that some aspects of the work we're doing will matter. Otherwise we're just hiding out."

"Me too. The damage that is happening right now is so severe it's hard to comprehend what the future will look like."

"How far do you think you will go with this project?"

"I have no idea," Levi answers.

"Me either," Naomi says as she moves from the exercise bike to a pull up bar.

"I want to go home someday," Levi says. "I just don't know where to go."

They work out in silence for a few minutes.

"Naomi, can you tell me anything more about Secret Eden?"

"We all bring something unique in with us that will be needed for the times ahead, Levi." Naomi hops down from the pull up bar and shrugs tension out of her shoulders. "If we were normal, leading conventional lives, we wouldn't be here right now. We'd be part of the system that is absorbing the extreme changes instead of being out here on the periphery focused on rebuilding in the aftermath."

"What about the others in camp?"

"Before being called here Bart was working on a Louisiana reseeding project to build the coastline back into the Gulf by redirecting materials headed for landfills and depositing them in receding spaces instead. Once a stable layer was in place, wild grasses and sugarcane could be planted to help buffer hurricanes and flooding. Then their stalks and clippings could be harvested to generate biofuels to offset the transportation of organic matter and non-toxic building materials from salvage projects."

"Clyde is a medic who can also help us live off the land," she continues, "Sourcing food and natural folk remedies if we can't access pharmaceuticals. And Jody is an electrical engineer who is trying to mitigate the impact of the solar storms on complex equipment."

"My turn," Naomi smiles. "What's your read on Outlander and Mallory?"

"Outlander is someone who I'm glad is on our side. He has grit. Mallory is quiet and focused. I think this is down time for them. That they're dialed into what it's going to be like out there on the road when we leave here one day soon."

SHENANDOAH

Day 13

Levi sits at his desk processing a box of papers with statistics on remaining untapped natural resources in Montana and North Dakota. Through the screen door he sees Outlander walk up and tap on the frame.

"Got a minute?" Outlander asks.

"Sure, what's up?"

"I'm asking everyone to stop by and see Clyde today for a checkup. There's a lot goin' on out there. These are weird times."

"Ok. I'll head over in a bit," Levi says.

"And tell him the truth. Clyde is perceptive. Hold back or evade and you'll have a redo with me and Clyde."

"Got it. Any news from outside the park?"

"Some. A lot of people are arriving on neutral ground in the National Park System." Outlander pauses, "People are fleeing the city for the countryside. I'm about to head down to the visitor center. There are three buses on their way up. We don't have the resources to absorb them though. We'll help with a resupply and route them on."

An hour later Levi walks across the mountain top and knocks

on the cabin door to Clyde's small clinic.

"Levi, thanks for stopping by." Clyde ushers him into his office and motions to a chair. Stout with curly hair and black rim glasses, dressed in a checkered shirt, brown corduroy jeans, and dark suede desert boots, the camp medic looks more like a professor or librarian.

"Outlander said you wanted to chat."

"Yes, if that's all right."

"Yeah, that's fine."

"Okay," Clyde nods. "How are you eating?"

"Well. The food is good. Like a home cooked meal. I think Mallory is trying to fatten us up. And the exercise we've been doing in the mornings keeps my appetite up."

"Good," Clyde replies. "And how are you sleeping?"

"Um," Levi hesitates. "Not so good some nights. Vivid dreams."

"So how are you responding to that? What do you do when you can't sleep or wake up rattled."

"It depends. The first night here I opened the cabin door and just let the mountain air in until the vibe was soothed away. When I was on the road this past year I would often just sit outside in nature and stare out into the night and take deep breaths until I felt centered. Last night I smoked a cigarette and sipped on whiskey."

"That's all fine, Levi. Sleep is elusive for many people even during normal times." Clyde adjusts his glasses. "And how are you feeling?"

"I don't know. Out of sorts I guess." Levi shrugs, knowing the first two questions were warm ups and to beware because this is the only question that matters to Clyde and Outlander. "It was like this the past year though. Everything upended."

"Go on, please continue," Clyde encourages. "This is just a conversation."

"I just try to focus on the day, man. The tasks at hand and my research. Sunrise to sunset and a little later into the evening hours." Levi breaks eye contact and looks out the window at moss rocks and thin windswept trees. "I also try to find something good in each day. Something new. Or something familiar. But something that feels good to counter balance anything that is not."

"What sustained you on the road?" Clyde asks. "You left your whole life behind."

"Yes, a lot a of good things. But I was also restless. Not fully connected to what I was meant to do with my life and attributes. So when I left it was to protect those around me and to protect me so that I could return home someday. Or at least somewhere close by. When I was on the road I was often calm. More relaxed driving down a highway I had never been on before heading towards a park I always dreamed of seeing, than I was back home in my normal routine. So to answer your question, I embraced the journey. Not every hour or every day. But most of the time."

"Good." Clyde smiles as he gets up and grabs a cola from the fridge. "Want one?"

"No, thanks."

Clyde settles back into his chair and takes a sip of his drink before swiveling his chair and setting the can on the desk where it begins to sweat onto the wooden surface.

"Let's get back to your time on the road. How often did you feel anxiety or down? Or ever?"

"In the wilderness, never. When I was in nature and the parks, pain and loss and fear of failure were grounded." Levi stares at Clyde for a long moment while he collects and chews on the words he wants to use. "That view flips in a city if I linger too long. It starts to drain me. Quickly. I'm burned out on city life. Give me the woods, and fresh air, birds in the trees, rain, and I can exist. Better than that, I can thrive."

"You know we will be passing through cities at some point," Clyde warns. "And they will be more volatile than ever."

"I know. As long as it is a pit stop I'll be fine. Just don't ask me to move there."

Clyde smiles and reaches to take another sip of his soda. "Why the fear of failure?"

"I always defined success as happiness as long as I was able to pay my bills and have a little money left over at the end of the month. Being unhappy at a job made me feel like a failure. I liked what I was doing this past year. The manual labor. Working with my hands during the day. Pursuing creative projects at night when my body was tired and my mind was alert. I worry sometimes about that balance flipping. I don't want to go back to sitting at a desk behind a computer." Levi catches the thought. "Well, things have changed. At least the dread of having to sit at a desk instead of being out and about still holds true."

"I know the feeling. I like being a nurse and I'm good at it," Clyde says. "It's important that people know what they are good at. But I also need nature. My beloved wife and I…," Clyde pauses and Levi sees his throat gulp and clamp down on emotion. "She passed recently."

"I'm sorry, Clyde."

"Thank you. Second bout with cancer. Amazing woman. We were high school sweethearts."

Levi waits while Clyde's distant thoughts return to the moment.

"We loved being outdoors on the weekends and found a shared hobby of growing heirloom seeds in our garden. We actually generated a nice side revenue stream. But when she passed it wasn't the same. So I channeled that energy into going into the woods and learning to forage. To try and do things the way the pioneers had to in order to survive. That's why I'm here."

Levi stands and walks to a window looking out over the woods and the meadow below camp. "You've got essential skills for the situation we are now in."

"Do you pray?" Clyde asks.

"Yes, all the time. Especially on those days."

"Good." Clyde removes his glasses and uses a small cloth to clean the lenses. "Wanna talk about Florida?"

"Nope," Levi says with an edge in his voice.

"Outlander said you had a side mission before arriving here. One that might be weighing on you. What happened in Florida?"

"Tell Outlander that if he wants to know he can come ask me himself."

"Okay. Last question, Mr. Wolff. What do you think is happening?" He motions up to the ceiling, implying through it. "The solar storms, the power outages. What do you think this means?"

"Different people will see it different ways. For me, it is a signal that the Information Age is over, and that the Age of Sustainability has arrived," Levi says. "And with all new ages, nothing will ever be the same."

SHENANDOAH

Day 14

Levi sits in the lodge dining room finishing a lunch plate of meatloaf, mashed potatoes, peas, and fried okra.

Outlander enters, loads up a plate from the buffet and takes a seat across from him. "Feeling okay? You look a little pale."

"Just thinking about what is happening out there. It's a lot to process. The suffering. The despair." Levi takes a deep breath, exhaling slowly. "The rapid change."

Outlander nods understanding.

"One time on the road I passed through Happy, Texas," Levi says. "Where tall telephone poles stuck in the golden grass like giant tobacco stained toothpicks. The line marching and fading into the horizon as it connected the countryside to civilization. Later that day I was heading to Dalhart and looked off to the west. A dark grey sky was moving in over the plains. Ominous in its approach. I debated pushing on until tornado sirens started to sound. So I turned around in the middle of the highway and headed back to the little town I had just passed through. A place called Vega.

"I parked at the town square and hopped out. The air became still and energized with the flicker of lighting and the rumble of thunder. Locals were descending on the municipal building. I grabbed a backpack and left everything else in the truck. Inside, the dispatcher told us a tornado had been spotted in the area and to move to the high school. I turned to a lady standing next to me and said I wasn't from around there and asked where the high school was. She said to just follow her. Then hesitated and said to just hop in with her. So I did."

Outlander begins to eat and listens patiently while Levi talks.

"Far from home, I walked into that school as the people of Vega gathered. They welcomed me in and I sheltered there as a traveler just passing through. I didn't know what I would have left after the storm passed but I was at least safe under the reinforced roof and walls. There was a sense of community present. People looking out for people, doing the right thing in a tense situation. And through a window, I watched the storm's fierce winds as hail fell and the tornado churned through nearby pastureland, sparing the town as it moved east.

"I remember walking outside after the sirens ended. The sky was the color of a bruise and a rainbow was arching over Route 66. When I got back to the town square and climbed in my truck after saying thank you's, I felt centered." Levi takes a sip of ice tea. "I hope that there are a lot of resilient places out there right now."

Outlander forks a bite of meatloaf into mashed potatoes and chews. "For today, try to push what is happening out there beyond Shenandoah away. What matters here and now is that you were on a list of people with ideas that correlate with how to rebuild an aspect of society after a collapse. The paradigm was already dying. We didn't know how or when, but we knew a collapse was coming. The math was irrefutable. Debt ghosting companies into the economy that do not exist. No employees. No products. Just liabilities." His eyes crease with focus. "You couldn't repair what existed before but you can help lay a foundation for what will come after."

"How?" Levi asks.

"This all happened fast. Various orders and emergency plans went out. And there was no consensus on how to react. Competing ideas are in motion that may collide." Outlander takes a swig of cola and rattles the ice cubes around in the fizz. "In order for America to survive, the Constitution has to survive. Your tangible currency model is just one of many aspects of Secret Eden that could prevent concentrations of power by dispersing sustainability. Each national park has research units working on various projects. And yours isn't the only currency model being compiled. There is redundancy in place."

"Okay," Levi says, "but how do we know we're the good guys?"

"We're not. Secret Eden is neutral. If anyone attacks us then they are operating out of bounds." Outlander glances out the window as a jeep crests the road and parks outside the lodge. "That's Jody. You met her yet?"

"No, not yet."

"We'll talk more later." Outlander nods to the door. "Go help her unload. She's got something for you. I think you'll like it."

Levi walks outside into the crisp mountain air, stoic as he wonders what the days ahead will be like, and whether he will be able to reconcile a sense of place in them. When he reaches the jeep, Jody is pushing aside a blue tarp to reveal a stack of grey cloth, the floral tattoos running up her arms contrasting with the dullness of the cargo. She is rail thin with hazel eyes bloodshot with fatigue, short spiky blonde hair, and a pale pallor from not spending enough time outdoors.

"Hi. I'm Levi. May I lend a hand?"

She nods and smiles through a gloss of plum colored lipstick. "I'm Jody."

"They said you've been out working with the Tennessee Valley Authority."

"I've been trying to guard the hydro electric generators in the dams by placing mat shields to block electromagnetic damage." She points to the stack of grey cloth. "These nets are lead and carbon composite weaves for the vehicles. I don't know if they'll work but it's better than nothing. Want one?"

"Definitely." He points to his truck parked on the edge of the row of cabins just down from the road. "I've got some extra supplies that I could trade for."

"That's not necessary," she says.

"I'd like to. My truck won't do me much good if it gets fried."

"Okay. Let's get these unloaded first." Jody reaches into the back of the jeep and starts handing him a stack of fabric at a time. "They can be dropped in the lobby."

Levi takes the packages and walks them inside the lodge in intervals.

A few minutes later Jody hands him the last one. "This is yours. You'll need this when we go roaming out there. Got time for me to show you how to attach it?"

"Sure. And thank you." As they walk down the stone sidewalk towards his vehicle Levi asks, "So how is it out there beyond the park boundary?"

"A lot of people are sheltering in place, waiting to see what happens. Local law enforcement and military units are deployed. They're trying to keep the roads open and the people moving as long as possible." Jody says and pauses. "We are in a race against time. Once the fuel supplies are used up, blockades will form."

"How much time do you think we have?" Levi asks.

"Not much. Days most likely. A few weeks at best. It's going to take impacted areas a really long time to stand back up. The more local people are, the more they will work together for their community. The small towns will fare much better than the big cities. They know each other. Compassion will be more abundant. They're not strangers."

They reach his pickup truck and Jody unfolds the net.

"It works like a blanket but instead of tucking corners there are clasps for the tires." Jody maneuvers around the hood while Levi pulls along the sides to the tailgate. "Each corner has a chain to funnel the current off the surface and into the metal links which wrap the rubber tires." She slips the corners over the tires until they each wear chains with a spike protruding from the ends. "Then you ground it like pitching a tent." She shoves the spike into the soft dirt ground around each of the front tires. "Got it?"

"Got it," Levi replies. "Makes sense."

"Good," Jody says. "Now the back. Your turn."

Levi moves to the tailgate, pulls the corners, unwinds the chains, clasps the tires, and spikes the ground. "What if we're on pavement?"

"Then just lay the spike on the ground. It'll send the charge. But if the wind is blowin' then you'll need to make sure those corners stay fastened. Especially on the front tires. Otherwise you could have trouble."

Levi steps back and surveys the grey net covering his truck.

"I would recommend leaving that in place until it's time to leave," she says.

"You've simulated this? It works?"

"Yes, we've simulated it." Jody sighs and opens a packet of bubble gum. "But this is the real thing. And it's different. Ethereal. More advanced than we can comprehend."

"How so?" Levi asks.

"We don't know yet," she says, shaking her head. "You'll have to talk to Outlander for anything beyond that. It's classified." She looks at him, pale, tired, driven. "I heard about the work you and Naomi are doing. A different way to store value that balances the old with the new. What do you see in all this, Levi?"

"The solar flares and auroras are scratching darkness across the surface of the Earth. Towers of Babel all across the world are going dormant. The technology inside them tumbling down," he says and stares into the forest. "Electric language is no longer flowing. Scattered spoken words are traveling local. Civilization is being unplugged. That's what I see. We're in the wild now."

SHENANDOAH

Day 15

Levi sits at his cabin desk late at night organizing notes and numbers from the boxes he carved through that day with Naomi. His left hand moves the pen across the pages in an arched indrawn paw style of writing. He likes being left handed in a right handed world. It has taught him to be a shape shifter within a framework that he was not designed for.

He feeds a postcard into the Corona typewriter to ink a letter home. When he finishes, he flips the card over to the daytime image of Daytona, Florida with its main avenue of dilapidated aqua neon lit hotels lining the beautiful coast like meth stained teeth. He plucked it from a desk drawer filled with a stack of red herring souvenir postcards from around the country that came in on a resupply. Everyone in camp got a parcel of blank cards pre stamped with the images' local ZIP codes.

The Corn Palace in Mitchell, South Dakota. A statue of the Jolly Green Giant in Blue Earth, Minnesota. Unclaimed airline baggage outlets in Scottsboro, Alabama inviting bargain hunters. Wild eyed bleach blond carnies playing a decaying piano in Venice Beach, California on a sidewalk in front of a tattoo parlor and an oddity museum. An assortment of random postcards waiting for his thoughts in the coming days. Or to gamble with over card games at night in their spare time. Outlander told Levi that the postcards were also being used to send coded messages to the other national parks. Reminding him that there is usually a catch, usually a ruse.

Levi extinguishes the lamp and rests his chin on his arms as he stares out into the night, blinking away fatigue from dimming eyes. Tethered to the image of an empty bunk waiting on him in the Cheaha Wilderness as he falls asleep on the desk.

Sixty miles away in Spotsylvania at a rural thoroughbred horse farm, Senator Ian Nix steps into his oak paneled office wheeling an oxygen canister. Each breath inside his decaying lungs a low wheeze. He coughs, then winces as the movement in his chest seems to shake something loose. He removes a kerchief from his grey tailored suit and dabs at his mouth before settling into a plush burgundy leather chair behind his desk.

He is a tall thin man who came of age as a paramilitary operative in the revolutionary filled jungles of Central America when he was chased and found half dead in quicksand and hanging onto life by clinging to the roots of a tree on the slimy edge of a pond. Rebels had chased him into the cement like vat and left him there to die, laughing and poking him with sticks as leeches suctioned themselves across his body. A recon unit that eventually stumbled upon him recalled that they went through a pack of cigarettes burning the leeches off his skin. Afterwards the reports said he looked like a dehydrated voodoo doll.

Then the legend grew. Adversaries in Europe grew to fear him as their spies began to turn up in public places with garrotes tied around their necks like bowties and titanium ice picks speared in the center of their foreheads like a kabob. The slim casino poker card that they would find on each victim, always the same. A cyclops skeleton walking among tombstones, dragging the leg of a corpse.

Ian Nix remained in the shadows for two decades until four federal employees were all found dead within a week of one another in the book stacks of various libraries around the capital. Necks snapped and silenced bullets to their hearts by the hands of Clay "Coffin Man" Donegal and Barrick Akkad. During a time when dangerous national security leaks were regularly occurring in various government agencies.

Surveillance from Nix's espionage unit which was brought in to help, uncovered that all four suspects had a similar routine. Stopping off at gas stations owned by the same man every so often and playing the lottery. Nix matched the selected lottery numbers to card catalogue book registries at local libraries where the rogue federal employees would deposit stolen documents deep in the stacks among forgotten texts. Then the gas station owner would retrieve the files, replace them with cash, and sell the secrets to the highest bidders on the dark web.

Nix's orders were to apprehend, not eliminate. Favors were called in. Nix was forced into retirement. Clay and Barrick were sent abroad into the asymmetrical War on Terror. The private sector beckoned and Nix helped assemble an international network of paramilitary security contractors for contracts in overseas third world and fourth world hellholes.

And during that time a Virginia state senator died from a heart attack. Ian Edward Nix, former spy and part owner of a private security firm with contracts and contacts throughout the world, ran in the special election, and narrowly won.

When the Aurora Terra arrived from the ether of space, his private army began returning home through various points of entry. And soon he will set them loose under order to weed out the Americans serving the Defcon Denver fallback plan, instead of the malleable Potomac Guard in the Jenkins Heights area of New Rome. Swelling their ranks along the way with desperate civilians trying to just survive the blackout.

Clay Donegal knocks and enters the office dressed in all black and wearing combat boots. His scraggy beard shaved, his long hair cut into a menacing mohawk. A pistol in his hands. "Good evening, sir."

Ian Nix motions him forward. "How long have we known each other?" he wheezes.

"A long time. Throughout many lands in a wilderness of mirrors," Clay says as he settles into a chair on the other side of the desk and places the pistol on the armrest.

For the past two years Clay operated out of villa set on a lush hillside in Switzerland along the shores of Lake Lucerne where Mount Pilatus juts across the horizon like a giant stone jaw. Often marveling at the fact that the majority of the population of the small canton nation could be shuttled deep into the Swiss Alps's bedrock carved tunnels within a matter of days, burrow, and not have to emerge for years from the subterranean, nuclear proof mountain bunkers.

Clay resisted the urge to reject his orders and disappear inside the chaos of a world already in self destruct mode, and now changing under the retrograde force of the Aurora Terra's bursting solar flares. Instead he returned stateside to wage a shadow war. Far away from the neutral crossroads of secret Switzerland where he hunted down white collar fugitives from the law, interrogated them, and seized their accounts for a slice of the bounty, before ending them. Now, Coffin Man is speaking with his mentor for the final time as humanity enters a Larium dream.

Nix removes an exotic mahogany wood tarot card sourced from the Cyclops Mountains in Papua New Guinea. The intricate paint and carved etchings depict a one eyed skeleton walking through a jungle beneath a sky holding the stars of the Ophiuchus constellation, the 13th Zodiac. Birds of paradise in the trees shielding their young with wings and plumes. Tattered flags from fallen nations lay at the skeleton's trampling feet. In the skeleton's bony hand, he holds a celestial globe of warring constellations. The tarot's most macabre image, a snake coiled around the skeleton's spinal cord with its tail piercing the heart and its reptilian head poking through the eye socket of the cyclops skull.

"This is yours now," Nix says as he slides the XIII death card across the surface to Coffin Man.

Clay Donegal picks the card off the desk and secures it in a pocket of his flak jacket vest. "Thank you, sir."

"What was your assessment of Shenandoah? Can they be lured into the reaper's swing?" Nix asks.

"They're secure on high ground. But vulnerable if hit with strength in numbers and the element of surprise," Donegal answers with cold eyes. "I didn't get a good look around. The sheriff was edgy. Denied my request to bed down for the night. But that's okay. I'll be seeing him again real soon." Coffin Man slides a national park pamphlet across the desk to Nix. "This simple map will get us there. Didn't appear that any new structures have been built, just modification and fortification to the visitor center."

"This mysterious work going on in the national parks. It's a volunteer project. No need to move too soon and show our hand," Nix explains in a low voice as he fumbles with a cigarette while trying to decide if he should light or not. "Natural attrition will reduce the ranks without any interference. But once their number is set, you will need to strike with the Erebus team in the countryside at will and without mercy." Nix reaches for a crystal vase instead and pours Scotch into two glasses, pushing one to Donegal. "Anyone serving Defcon Denver is marked for death. We need centralized power, not dispersed fiefdoms."

"Akkad confirmed he is embedded with the western militia in an isolated rugged region of northern Idaho. They will split up in ten days," Clay explains. "One team launching out of the Lost River to intersect with the Snake River running through Hells Canyon National Recreation Area. The other unit will cross into Montana, then ride the Anaconda Railroad through the Sleeping Giant Wilderness and take the Beartooth Scenic Byway to attack."

"All teams should utilize the designated empty government buildings found in every mid-sized or major city." Nix takes a deep sip of Scotch and adjusts the oxygen tube in his nose to breathe pure air into his ruined lungs. "The idle doomsday hotels are stocked with provisions. A detailed list of where to find them is in the top left drawer of my desk. Barrick has the same list."

"I will make copies for the men," Clay replies.

"Superstition can be a most effective camouflage," the old man offers a wry smile. "It is rather easy to create a hidden floor when the elevator number pad skips the thirteenth floor. Especially when over time, people have been subconsciously programmed to overlook such a detail."

Clay Donegal lifts the pistol from the chair's armrest and lays it across his lap. He runs a hand through his black mohawk, steeling his resolve as undertaker.

Nix lights a cigarette and stares at the burning stick of mortality. "Do you ever wonder if the reason Adam and Eve were told not to eat from the Tree of Knowledge of Good & Evil was so that they would get hungry and dine on the serpent when it came along?"

Coffin Man stays silent as the rhetorical question hovers.

"Well, it's too late to go back now." Senator Nix removes the oxygen tube and lets it drop like a pendulum, its plastic umbilical cord swinging his final seconds of life. His ravaged body almost at its end. "I'm tired and in constant pain. I'm ready. Please go ahead and do it. Then set them loose. Lead your Erebus team west. Infiltrate. Take back the old ways."

Clay Donegal nods once with acceptance of his duty. "Welcome to the void, sir. May you find peace in the center of stillness." Then Coffin Man shoots his mentor twice in the heart with a hollow point double tap to end the suffering.

SHENANDOAH

Day 16

Naomi and Levi hike along the Appalachian Trail under tree canopies spreading earth toned fall colors through the leaves. Their recent days passing in a blur. Boxing pads cushion the blows from full contact hand to hand training. Medic sessions teach their fingers how to probe and heal wounds likely to be incurred in the field. Physical training regimens keeps their bodies sore, and numb in the lucky spots. Target practice at outdoor firing range next to the visitor center fills the ground with spent ammunition shells and cakes the air with cordite. Disassembling and reassembling handguns, rifles, shotguns, and machine guns scrapes away soft skin on their hands and replaces it with rough calluses. Field maneuvers teach them how to move in offensive and defensive formations. And day trips along Skyline Drive and off into nearby towns in modified all-terrain vehicles train the operatives on how to travel through simulated urban combat zones.

Days begin at sunup and end late into the evening. Sleep remains a coveted luxury. An air raid siren located in a foxhole atop the visitor center releases banshee decibels at the worst possible hours, jarring the volunteers with its insomnia inducing wail, flinging them out of bed on reflex to assemble as a tribe at the lodge flagpole at any hour, regardless of the weather conditions.

Levi and Naomi have processed through half the stack of data boxes, resulting in the gradual expansion of narrow walking paths inside each of their cluttered minimalist cabins.

They hear a noise in the brush and spot a doe watching them. The white tailed deer studies them for a moment before becoming at ease with their presence and dips her head into grass blades beneath her hooves, pulling chunks up into her mouth, jaws chewing and chomping as cute ears bob with the motion. They stop and sit atop the log of a fallen tree that lays a wooden line across the soft ground. Levi traces his hand along a patch of spongy emerald green moss growing atop flakes of tree bark. Naomi unzips her daypack and hands over baggies of dried fruit and shelled mixed nuts. They rest and snack in silence as time flows through the forest of Shenandoah and the deer silently disappears from view.

"The blue in your eyes is elusive. I can see it but I can't take it out of your eyes and put it in my mind's eye and hold it there." Naomi looks over at him, dark circles beneath her eyes, "It fades every time I try. My eyes," she says, "are the color of these ferns. I look around this forest and see my hue everywhere. Your eyes though, I only see the color near the ocean."

"I miss the coast," he says. "How are you sleeping?"

"Not so well. Nightmares. I wake up and draw them sometimes to try and capture them in this realm so that they will go away." She sighs. "Some nights I just sit up in bed until dawn processing data from the boxes, avoiding sleep."

"That's not good," he says. "You need to maintain a reserve of energy for the unknown."

"I know. I'm trying." Naomi reaches into the backpack and

withdraws a canvas scroll bound with a hair ribbon. She pulls the ribbon off and uses it to tie her blonde hair up in a ponytail. "This is last night's dream." She hands the scroll to him. "I just want to rest here for a little while if that's okay."

"Of course. Take your time. I'll keep watch."

Naomi turns away, lays a blanket down on the forest floor and reaches out to run her fingers along the ferns. "I feel better out here. It allows me to get tired." Then she tucks her body into a ball and tries to fall asleep.

Levi unrolls the image captured from her nightmare. Marks of vivid oil based crayons spread over the rectangle mat of rough cut canvas to reveal a dark figure perched on a rock in front of a campfire in the wilderness. Shadows of night obscure the features of his face. A stained knife in his palm drips blood into a pool at his sandaled feet. Stars hover in the sky above a pit of stones where a stick of wood mounts two hearts on a rotisserie that roasts the still organs above the flames. A disemboweled lion and wolf sleep beside each other as companions in death. Blood scars trace a thick mane of yellow fir and shorter nape of grey hair where the knife severed vital vessels. Trauma rests on their paws in a hollow mush of tissue and bone. Claws from the lion and wolf paws hang from a necklace on the killer's neck. And the dark man's red eyes reflect into the orange flames in the pit as they fixate on the cooking hearts he is about to devour with his drooling hand.

Shudders ripple through Levi as he analyzes the haunting canvas, wondering if he is staring at a premonition or a piece of dark dream art. He rolls the painting back up and sets it in her daypack. "Is this a recurring dream?"

"I'm not sure. I don't always remember them, just the emotions," her voice faint. "That image was just there in the dream as a vibration, so I included it."

"And the man in the shadows?"

"I don't know that either."

When he glances back at Naomi resting in peace, he notices the edge of another scroll sticking out of her backpack. He reaches for it, unties the burlap string and removes a lithograph canvas. Levi carries it across the woods to a bluff overlooking the town of Lydia down in the valley, where rolling foothills of farmland contain fields of hay, assorted crops, apple orchards, small vineyards, bails dotting the pastures, and the orange dots of a pumpkin patch. Tiny one lane roads weave themselves through assorted hollows and coves where it seems as if the families with their grain silos and tin roof red barns can just block the roads leading in and let the days pass by. He stares at the pastoral innocence from above and feels a stab of envy at those who are still able to experience the fleeting world that he left behind.

Then he spots a deep blue butterfly with a battered wing laying still in the crevice of a lichen covered rock. Unable to fly and feed, windswept to a final resting spot from its caterpillar birth. Levi touches the butterfly and lifts it gently in his palm. Dark dust falls onto his hand as he tries to smooth the broken wing. He places it back down on the resting place and tries to brush the indigo butterfly ink from his fingertips. But the color remains embedded on his skin as if marking him for touching beauty.

He unrolls Naomi's drawing. The image is of Skyline Drive's faint yellow line cutting a meandering path through a lush forest. In the distance, a tornado funnel bends across the horizon as spiked tendrils of lightning jolt the ground on the periphery. Levi holds the painting closer and spots a silhouette walking the road beside a sign reading I-〰. He stares at the saw blade symbol for a long time, wondering what the message is all about as the wind rustles the woods. He counts the rendered symbol's rising and falling pyramid stacked lines. Six up and six down. Twelve in all. Then Levi recalls entering the park along I-66. Interstate Aquarius. The current Zodiac age.

SHENANDOAH

Day 17

The sun rises over a distant ridge and slices the dawn over a meadow covered with morning dew. Outlander ties a blindfold over Levi's eyes in the back cab of a camp pickup truck as Mallory drives them out of the field across from the visitor center and onto Skyline Drive. Deprived of sight, nausea blooms in Levi with each directional change as if riding an unbound roller coaster. An hour later, she turns and drives down a slope into the woods along a ranger firebreak trail.

"Now you can open your eyes," Outlander says as the truck slows. "It's drop time tenderfoot."

Levi removes the blindfold and stands to fade the dizziness.

"The pattern will repeat itself today as the rest of our cabin row are deposited at various spots in the park," the sheriff explains. "Stay off the road if you happen to find it. If we catch you walking pavement while out on patrol, we'll drop you back at the start."

Mallory leans out the driver window. "Welcome to wilderness survival," she says smiling. "Out you go."

Levi lowers the tailgate and hops down onto a cushion of ground in the middle of dense Blue Ridge forest.

"Here's your map and compass." Outlander tosses both objects.

Levi surveys the drop zone as the pickup hiccups its way back up the trail. Alone in a disturbed forest, he unfolds his map and places the compass on it, watching the needle wobble and then steady itself. Levi spares a few minutes to take in the feel of the area. With the way back to camp an unknown, Levi turns a full three hundred and sixty degrees. When he spots a distant ridgeline jutting higher than the rest of the surrounding maze, he heads for it, ignoring the map and compass for the time being.

An hour and a half later he reaches the selected ridge and stares out over Shenandoah Valley. He uses the same method again and heads towards the next point, alternating cross country running with hiking, never stopping, always keeping in motion. He follows the terrain for hours. His clothes become drenched with sweat and his dry throat receives only a few drops of saliva.

Levi finds a stone marker around midday buried in the dirt at a trailhead. He identifies the nodes and heads southwest on the Appalachian National Scenic Trail. After a few miles of steady hiking, he finds a stream occupied by four large crows. They scatter to the trees with angry squawks and then fall into a silent intelligence as if half attuned to the netherworld. Levi watches the crows as he lays flat on the ground on the edge of the stream and drinks cold mountain water from the nozzle of a charcoal filtered survival straw, their sleek profiles pointed in different directions, a loyal pack watching. Once has his fill and catches his breath, he moves back from the stream and continues on through the woods. Slowing once to give a coiled timber rattler napping on the edge of a pond a respectful wide berth.

Two hours later, Levi enters a clearing filled with vines of ivy. A chipmunk darts past his feet and seeks refuge in a nearby hole. He takes a few minutes to rest. Then he starts to run again through a grove of tall trees. The thin path crosses a low creek bed filled with smoothed rocks, rises up a hill in alternating switchbacks, and curves around a bend where it straightens out into a long line.

Thick foliage juts up along the side, masking the view below the trail. His pace slows to a jog for a half mile to avoid tripping through a section of raised tree roots. Then the brush clears away. The trail passes under a lush tree canopy where shades of light and shadow fall across lichen covered stones and topsoil the color of ground nutmeg. The place is eerily silent, as if something slashed its vocal chords. Then Levi's periphery vision registers a large dark shape off to his right.

He turns and halts as he spots a black bear moving across the ground in a trajectory that aims their paths for a secluded convergence. Levi only has a brief second to view the young full grown male before the majestic creature detects an intruder's presence, straightens up, lifts its ears, and swivels alert. The black bear and Levi Wolff lock mutually wide eyes.

Awareness of the situation overrides alarm and awe as Levi raises his hands high to increase his profile. The bear reacts in an instant by swerving and dashing away. But as it runs fast and powerful, it steals a quick glance back at him as if reconsidering. Levi counters by speaking gibberish in a loud deep voice. The black bear turns its brown face away and increases its speed as it vanishes from view, sending trailing noise back through the forest as it tears through brush and travels deep into the woods.

The humbling encounter is over in less than half a minute. Realizing he has outstayed the moment, he resumes running along the trail with veins pumping a river of adrenalin, looking back every so often, mindful of any odd sounds off in the distance as he follows the contours of the trail passing underfoot. Along the way Levi finds an energy and speed that surprises him and makes him long for the ability to tap into such endurance at will. A few miles up trail he stops and bends over, placing hands on thighs as he shovels breath in protesting lungs. When his heart rate slows a little he shakes his head and smiles, feeling energized.

A half hour later, he stands atop the strata of Stony Man Summit. Levi leans his head back and watches cotton clouds glide across the blue sky. He stays up there for a while, surveying a panorama where the mountains slope into rolling hills that disappear into the horizon of West Virginia. After recharging, he pulls himself away from the tranquility and repeats the grueling process of running and hiking until his body is utterly depleted of energy to the point where hunger, thirst and fatigue poke their way into every muscle and thought by the time the sun sets and dusk falls over the countryside in an afterglow.

Levi hits a new trail and jogs for another hour, ignoring an internal warning to stop and rest until stars can be seen through the trees in the sky above. He finally stops at a mammoth oak tree that forces the path to bend a semicircle around the towering obstacle. Yearning for nourishment, he digs into dirt near the trunk of the tree and uses night eyes to find a handful of plump grub worms. Levi bites through their stark white skin with a slight cringe of anticipation as crickets grind their legs in a guttural rhythm in the branches above. Mushy protein moves across his tongue and his taste buds associate the earthy, nutty taste with ground peanuts. Then he tucks his head into his knees to stay alert and warm while the temperature drops and his body rests.

Late that night, noise from something moving close awakens him from a light sleep. His back stiffens against the trunk of the oak tree and he peers into the forest. His first thought is that the black bear from late afternoon has tracked him down. While he waits and listens, Levi fights a voice telling him that he should have never left Alabama, that if he stayed he would be in a comfortable bed right now at a homestead with human dangers that he was better programmed to address. Levi catches the rebelling thought and looks up for a moment at the bright moon, wondering for an instant if the orb is a giant typewriter ball in the sky whose craters align to the galaxy's stars like inverted Braille, before lowering his eyes as the sound grows closer.

The glowing eyes of a grey fox appear a few feet away and meet Levi's. The fox lifts its delicate nose in the air and gets a whiff of intrusion. Then it changes course and creeps off into the night. Levi Wolff rises into the moonlight with subsiding alarm. Knowing there is no way he can go back to sleep now, he stumbles through the darkness, following the trail as best he can with sweat burned eyes.

After a while, he crosses a narrow wooden bridge that he recognizes and pauses on the rail to observe the soothing flow of a stream with stars shimmering in its water, the starlight arriving from unfathomable distances. The moon moving in the coursing water, bending along its curves, the circumference of its orb waning in small degrees along its edges in the stream's nocturnal flow down the mountain, as the full moon's gravitational pull adds height to tides on distant coastlines. Levi silently wondering if maybe lunar gravity makes the mystery of Pi a living number whose radius extends to Earth, bound to repeat in inanimate objects, but patterned when viewed by how it is found in nature across a lunar cycle in the ebb and flow of ocean tides bending in the moonlight against a baseline average.

He crosses the wooden bridge over the stream and keeps moving through the forest, remembering how the symbol for Pi resembles the stubby heavy stone slab graves of ancient nomads found in the Golan Heights of Israel above the Sea of Galilee near the mystical mountain city of Tzfat and fortress of Gamla.

The wandering man from Alabama stops only once more, to stand on a tree stump, breathe deep, listen, and feel the subtle energy in a wooden echo of how tall the stature once was.

Levi enters camp soon after with a weary step in his sore legs, spotting Outlander, Mallory, and National Guard soldiers from the barracks standing around a bonfire below the visitor center that lights a path in for the stragglers. Rolled sleeping bags are dispersed through the meadow like bales of hay. Naomi, Jody, and Clyde are already bedded down along mats and napping.

He snags a sleeping bag and winces from protesting muscles as he stoops down, unties the straps and unrolls it with a bowling motion. Then he climbs on the mat and lays back, covering his face with the nook between his forearm and bicep. Listening to the fire squeeze moisture from the burning logs with a low whine punctuated by pops that mimic cracking knuckles. Aromatic smoke coursing in the wind that moves over the meadow where the operatives are scattered like tranquilized animals. Minutes later Levi is in a deep sleep as Outlander stares into the fire thinking about old missions in doomed places while a soldier takes out a harmonica and whistles a soft pioneer tune while they wait for a lost mechanic to wander into camp.

FIRE
13·14

SHENANDOAH

Day 18

The camp gathers at dusk in the lodge's cozy downstairs tavern. Levi and Naomi slide into a booth with Clyde and Jody, who is antsy and tapping her nails on the table.

"It was a long day at the clinic. A lot of the people heading back into D.C. are wounded." Clyde sips on gin over ice with a squeeze of lime.

"I've seen it too when traveling between TVA sites," Jody says. "Things are rough out there. You can see it in their eyes."

"Has anyone heard any news from overseas?" Naomi asks.

Clyde shakes his head, drains the gin from his glass, and rattles the ice cubes.

"Bits and pieces of radio chatter gets through," Jody says. "But it's hard to verify the accuracy of the info."

"I haven't," Levi replies, "Not since the night the solar flares arrived when I was driving through the Mojave Desert." He shifts in his seat and winces at the protest from sore ribs courtesy of an agile kick from Mallory that morning during a sparring session.

"How is the currency work going?" Jody asks.

"We're done," Naomi says. "We finished processing the last of the boxes and typed up the final sheets of figures this morning after training."

Mallory enters the tavern and pulls a chair up to the table. "Outlander and Bart are on their way down."

They arrive carrying a long pine wood crate and set it on the low stage where acoustic singers would play on the weekends for tourists. Then Bart heads to the bar to pour two mugs of beer from a keg tap.

The operatives gathered around the table watch M4 submachine guns, .40 caliber pistols, steel bayonets, and ammunition canisters being removed from the crate.

"Everyone take one of each on your way out," Outlander says, "You'll need them for the journey ahead. Winter pea coats with patches sewn on the shoulders and leather gloves have been placed on the porches in front of your cabins." The sheriff of Shenandoah grabs a bar stool and sits under the dim lights. "There will be no going back to the life you left behind. It will only exist as a memory of the ways things were before. We won't be insulated in this sanctuary much longer. Soon we will be loading up and riding out into the chaos to join the other tribes of Secret Eden."

Bart hands him a mug of beer and Outlander pauses to take a sip.

"It has already begun for the distant national parks. They are on the move and folding into the continental area. They are inbound with each tribe reduced to a mobile platoon of operatives and soldiers."

"So what's the plan?" Jody asks.

"Each park is different. With their own unique projects and missions," Outlander answers. "Our first hop will take us to Great Smoky Mountains National Park where we will rendezvous with other tribes from our region. And then from there on to another farther and colder hop that will remain classified for now.

Tomorrow, pack your gear and get ready. The soldiers are field stripping the library as we speak, burning all classified materials. The Acadia, Cuyahoga and Congaree tribes are on their way. That is all for tonight. Grab your gear and some rest. Tomorrow will come early."

Levi pours a glass of whiskey at the bar and walks out the back of the den to the patio. He sinks into a rocking chair and listens for a while to crickets grinding conversations through the trees in the twilight.

When he finishes his drink he takes the spiral stairs back up to the lobby and drifts back to his cabin. Entering his room and leaving the lights off as he sits down at his desk and looks through the window to a tree branch swaying in the night breeze above a grove of moonlit ferns.

Feeling a blend of anticipation and mystery of what it will be like to be in motion again when he hears a knock and moves to open the door.

Naomi stands outside on the steps with tired eyes. "I can't sleep," she says with shyness. "And I don't want to be alone tonight."

He opens the door wider. "It will be good to have some company to keep me from brooding over thoughts of what's ahead."

Naomi enters the cabin and takes a seat on the edge of the bed, seductive in her fatigue. Her shorts rise higher on her slender legs. Full breasts snug under a tee shirt. Hair pulled up with a clip. Stray sand blonde strands falling over her face, partially masking her jade eyes.

Levi moves to the bed and sits beside her. Naomi turns to him and stares into his face. He pushes back her bangs and places his palm against the warm skin of her neck. "I'm glad you knocked," he says.

Naomi tucks her face into his chest. Then she lifts her chin and pecks Levi on the cheek. She leans back, looks into his eyes and softly kisses his cheek again, closer to his lips this time as he breathes in the scent of her citrus perfume. Naomi glides her lips to his mouth and kisses him. Her kisses taste like butterscotch candy as she melds her body to his.

Then she turns away from him, pulls the shirt up her back and lets it drop to the floor. She unclasps the bra and it falls off her back like a petal from a flower. Naomi lays an arm across her breasts and turns to face him. Levi watches shadows fall across the beautiful curves of her body as she snuggles into his arms and lays a hand on his heart. He wraps a warm blanket over them.

"Hold me," she whispers in a delicate voice. They stare out the window into the night, beyond the darkness and skeletal tree branches, past the sanctuary of Shenandoah, into a world growing ever more dangerous. Naomi runs her hand through his hair, pulling stress from his mind with each delicate movement.

Soon the tension builds and they undress each other and intertwine their desire in the night. The loneliness of their solitary lives fades away. Then afterwards Naomi cuddles against Levi as they fall into a relaxed sleep.

At dawn, Levi wakes from vivid and challenging dreams, the kind that seem to travel between dimensions. After gathering his hazy senses, he turns over and sees Naomi sleeping beside him. His hand brushes away strands of hair from her face as he leans on an elbow and watches her puffy lips melt into a smile before her eyes open.

Naomi purrs and stretches. "Hi," she says softly as she sits up against the headboard and tucks pillows behind her. "How much time do we have before training?"

"About an hour." He kisses her as dawn peers through the trees and begins to wake the forest.

Naomi's magnetic eyes study him. "You're different, Levi. It takes a little time to spot it but it's there. Like a subtle scar that wicks in and out of existence."

He shrugs, "I'm just me."

"What is it that happened to you in the past?" she asks as she lays a kiss on his lips. "How did you end up here?"

Levi pauses, hesitant, and looks away, not wanting to push her away with his words. His memory reluctantly walking backwards into the past. Naomi waits patiently, holding his eyes in hers. She senses his discomfort and scoots closer to him. He feels the exhale of her breath brush past his heart.

"I was poisoned." Levi tries to gather words from his past, recalling images and emotions that still rattle him. Then he begins to talk about the pain that altered his life path as he lays back into the arms of a beautiful woman that would see him differently once the story was finished being told. "I call it my lost year."

Levi recounts the day and night in Montgomery that ended with him falling down a trail next to the Alabama River, frozen in the sickness of an exotic potion of poison. Then he tells Naomi of his travels to heal. And ends with the tale of revenge three weeks ago along the Forgotten Coast.

"Did you see anything in the hallucinations that you carried out with you?" Naomi asks.

"Yes. Some."

"What?"

"I dreamed I was dying, and that opened up a gateway where I saw stuff that we're not supposed to see unless we're going over to that other side and not coming back," Levi says quietly. "It took me to both extremes of happiness and sadness. I also remember that the last thought I had before going into shock and being dragged into the coma was feeling like I couldn't breathe and was suffocating because my belly button is sewn shut."

Naomi reaches out her hand to hold his tightly.

He continues, "The journey pulled energy from me and that stolen energy powered the realm I was taken to. The coma took some time crawl out of. Eventually I was spit back into consciousness with no directions on how to find my way back to where I was before." He shakes his head slightly. "At times when I was on the road moving from park to park, I used to ask silent questions. Am I permanently damaged? Why do I hear music more clearly now?" He pauses. "Also, when I read the words *G-d* and *Israel* in a sentence, I feel a duality and combine them into a reminder that G-d is real."

Naomi patiently waits for him to continue.

"Over time I realized that I had been knocked off a routine trajectory in order to either die or awake to a more mystical existence. And sometimes I would wonder if the aura of the event was that of an angel or a demon."

"Perhaps both were present at that moment as a spiritual balance," Naomi says. "An angel standing nearby to witness you being put on the path your life was endowed for. And the demon there to put it all in jeopardy. Each playing their part in the battle for your soul."

"Possibly," Levi says. "I was different afterwards. More aware. More sentient. But changed for sure. The pain fell away in pieces over time. It was like each new place that I traveled to sewed a stitch in the wound. And I learned important things on the road."

"Like what?" Naomi asks softly as she turns his cheek to kiss him.

"That everyone has to walk their own spiritual path. And it can be lonely unless we're connecting with the heart of the journey."

"What else?" she asks.

"I learned to make important decisions quickly."

"For example?"

"Like right now. Here with you. I don't know what is going to happen in the days ahead, but I want it to happen with you. I like the way it feels to be near you, to be with you."

SAWTOOTH WILDERNESS

Day 19

Barrick Akkad sits on a ridge in dark woods beneath a night sky slowly turning with specs of starlight. A citizen band radio propped on a spruce log beside him and tuned to a pirate channel. He waits for a voice to arrive from across the Continental Divide, hoping the radio's twin has not been fried by the solar storms.

"Vania calling." Clay Donegal's cryptic voice finally wheezes through the transmission. "Over."

Barrick reaches for the CB radio's microphone. "How is he?"

"He's gone."

Barrick's jaw tightens. "Do we still have a green light?"

"Our mission remains."

"10-4. I understand. Over."

"How is the west side?" Clay asks.

"Shaky City and the Needle are still dark," Barrick shifts his dialect to trucker. "Lost Wages and the Sticker Patch are going dry. What about the east side?"

"Chaos. We vacate the outskirts of New Rome at dawn with claws out and en route," Clay matching the slang. "What's your 20, brother?"

"North of Spud Town."

"Affirmative," Clay replies. "After we draw blood, it's on to River City and through Hog Country to the home stretch."

"Ride the hammer lane along the big road."

"We'll be marching yardsticks and hunting along the way," Clay relays.

"See you in Geyser City." Barrick signs off.

"Copy that. Over and out."

Barrick turns the knob to a random channel and abandons the radio as he walks down the ridge to his team's isolated campsite in a valley connected to a one lane road winding around a lake. Dots of lantern light from RVs and tents pitched beside vehicles illuminating a serene calm that belies the volatile days ahead.

SHENANDOAH

Day 20

'I'm ready to go," Naomi says in the afternoon chill as she sits down on the porch steps in front of her cabin. "How 'bout you?" Her warm breaths puffing small chimneys.

"I don't know," Levi says as he readies supplies from his cabin to load up in his pickup truck tucked away at the end of the row beside his cabin. He stares out at distant lightning that licks the horizon with an electric tongue as storm clouds gather in the sky and creep in over the valley. "It depends on what we find out there on the road."

Wind rustles dying leaves of autumn from tree branches and floats them down to the ground as Naomi and Levi enter his cabin. They drop their guns and backpacks in a corner as winds press on the roof and windows as if trying to break in. Snowflakes begin to trickle down on the mountain top in the fading day's light.

Nearby, one hundred mercenaries drive out of Spotsylvania and head due west along a remote Virginia highway towards the border of Shenandoah National Park. When they arrive, they leave the pavement and move into a labyrinth of dirt trails that rise through the Blue Ridge Mountains. The men and women abandon their vehicles at the edge of the Dark Hollow Falls trail system, load expedition packs and trespass into the nature preserve in a long line. When the forest swallows them, they withdraw submachine guns from their packs, load ammunition magazines, and fasten sound suppressors to the gun barrels.

A few miles up the trail, the paramilitary force halts when they spot a mother bear and her cub moving through the forest. Coffin Man creeps forward, aims his silenced weapon and squeezes the trigger. The hind legs of the momma bear spasm as blood mists through the air. The bear roars and falls as her cub runs to safety. Coffin Man jogs up the trail towards his prey. The mother bear leaks a blood trail as her unwounded legs claw their way through the forest. He approaches and aims. The bear spins and her jaws unclasp in defensive fear. Coffin Man fires two shots into the female bear's vulnerable chest. Her head rocks awkwardly to the side, and the bear exhales a low growl as it slumps back and lays still.

The child cries. The brush fills with the sound of rushing feet. The cub appears in a clearing, wailing all the way to Coffin Man as it alternates glances between its mother and her killer. Coffin Man withdraws a hunter's knife from its sheath and flicks an experienced arm forward. The steel blade tumbles through the air and sinks in the cub's neck. It shrieks as blood pours out onto its black fur. It continues a death run a few more feet but the young body stumbles awkwardly down the trail and falls beside a rock. Crying softly, it turns towards its mother and tries to crawl to her. The cub's strength fails and it goes silent on the forest floor.

The mercenaries surround the black bears with unsheathed knives and begin removing trophy claws from the paws. "Bag the skulls," Coffin Man orders as he turns to the sky and surveys a grey wall of snow approaching the park from the west. "Our camouflage is here."

Up at the visitor center, guards with thick coats resting on their shoulders and scarves tucked tightly into the collars, pace to keep warm as a convoy of vehicles appears around a bend on Skyline Drive. When the convoy reaches the turn leading up to the lodge, the patrolling sentries stop the jeeps and check the patches on bulletproof vests before letting them pass. After sliding their way up, the vehicles reach the mountain top and park in front of the lodge. Passengers hop out into the cold air and move towards the empty cabins on the east side of camp as Mohegan Acadia and Joe Congaree break off and head west across the grounds and up the stairs to the room above the main lodge.

Outlander meets the Secret Eden sheriffs at the door with cups of hot apple cider in hand. The back wall of his room covered with a large map of America pockmarked with various colored pins that delineate areas of activity.

"Thorpe Cuyahoga and his team have been delayed," Mohegan says as she loops her hands into the shoulder straps of her vest. "We waited at the north gate barricade for as long as we could."

"Do you want to be there at the north gate to meet him when he arrives?" Joe says as he takes a sip of cider. "They may have wounded."

"Yes, of course," Outlander Shenandoah says as he puts on his coat and grabs a shotgun and rifle. "I'll take two vehicles down. Our camp medic and mechanic will be along for the ride just in case." He pauses at the doorway. "Get settled in. There's food in the dining room if you're hungry."

Outside he enters a wall of cold wind that pushes against him as he turns to the stretch of cabins adjoining the lodge. He knocks on three doors. "Mallory, you're with me in my truck. Bart and Clyde, grab your stuff and follow us. The Cuyahoga team has been delayed. There may be wounded arriving. In this weather it will be about two hours down and two hours back."

A few minutes later, a pickup truck and SUV drive down

from the lodge. Mallory riding in the shotgun seat next to her fiancé with an M4 between her knee and the center console. Bart following with Clyde and his medic kit beside him. When the two vehicles reach the bottom of the hill a National Guard soldier from the barracks approaches the vehicle. Outlander rolls his window down and cold wind gusts in. "Sergeant, you got five on duty down here?"

"Affirmative. Four on ground and one in the nest."

"I'm heading to the north gate to wait for the Cuyahoga tribe." Outlander says, "Wake up five more soldiers and put them on top of the hill in full gear."

"Yes, sir. Copy that. They'll be posted within ten minutes."

Outlander and Bart drive away and mash their vehicle hazard lights as they swing onto Skyline Drive, driving slowly at first while their eyes to adjust to the rhythm of the snow spilling across the windshield before speeding up.

Back beyond a hemlock tree line of the meadow, predators wait in the shadows and watch two lone vehicles pass by on a northern course and disappear around a bend in the alpenglow of the day's fading sun.

Inside Levi's cabin, Naomi removes a bottle of whiskey from her backpack and pours amber liquid into two tumblers as they watch the wind sways the trees outside and bend the branches. Naomi lifts her glass for a toast. "*L'chaim.*"

"And to the road ahead," Levi adds as their glasses kiss. "Let's get some rest. Tomorrow is going to be a long day."

An hour later, below the lodge and across the meadow, Coffin Man lowers a plastic face mask, raises a gloved fist to his troops and brings it down as an order to begin. Mercenaries emerge out of the woods wearing chalk colored arctic survival suits and jog through an open field of snow towards the visitor center complex, clutching submachine guns and moving forward in an arc across the snowy meadow.

The Shenandoah visitor center guards spot shapes rushing out of the blizzard. They raise their weapons to react with alarm. Muzzles flare from both sides unleashing bursts of gunfire. The windows of the visitor center burst and shatter panes of glass. Return fire spears the attackers with searing bullets, bending wounded bodies, and throwing some of the shock troops into shallow graves of snow.

A lone soldier on the roof of the visitor center fires into the mass of approaching shapes with one hand as his other hand furiously cranks an air raid siren's handle. An apocalyptic wail bellows out of the meadow while they fend off the attackers, unsure if the lodge will hear their warning through the snowstorm.

Levi is asleep with Naomi snuggled in beside him, her soft breaths brushing her bangs back and forth across the pillow as she holds his left forearm in a gentle grasp. But Levi's mind is elsewhere, walking in the wilderness of his dreams inside Hawaii Volcanoes National Park. Blending with the foliage atop a panoramic ridge as he nests in a swaying, sun coated hammock tied between a pair of rainbow eucalyptus trees with camouflage tiger striped bark.

Levi Wolff divides a heterochromatic stare between the dark almond earth of a rising mountain and the tumbling azure blue ocean. The hollow socket of Mount Kilauea's eye cries lava tears that slide through the jungle brush like fiery slugs, igniting vegetation all the way down until they tip into the cool ocean water and explode into vivid paint as they waft dull tones of sulfur smoke across the horizon like an eerie fog.

Inside the hammock of his dream, Levi feels tiny smiley face spiders trickle down from the tree behind his head and watches them form into a thin lemon peel line as they march down his forearm's light blue bloodlines to the palm of his left hand where he clutches a glass sphere wrapped in a piece of tattered paper. The bright translucent spiders swarm over the sheet, forming an undulating cluster of black dot Rorschach eyes with lipstick red smiles.

The mesmerizing little spiders smother the paper wrapped sphere. Until an air raid siren begins to wail from across the cascading ocean waves, turning his veins to cold slush. The yellow smiley face spiders scamper away, running down the hammock's woven mesh web and trickling up the rainbow eucalyptus tree beyond his feet.

Levi shudders and lifts his left hand which holds the glass globe wrapped in a faded letter. He turns it in his palm as he reads a strand of indigo typewriter ink ringing the globe's equator. *A storm is coming. You need to hurry.* As soon he absorbs the familiar words, the tattered paper catches in the wind, rising like a jellyfish moving through water, drifting up and fluttering out to sea. Levi looks into the distance as the banshee siren's decibels pierce his eardrums.

An old wooden ship with wind puffed squares of white cloth sails parallel to the shore, bobbing as waves splash across its hull, showering surf over the sides and across an abandoned deck. A long plank of wood hanging off the ship like a diving board of discipline, loses its nails and falls in the swallow of the ocean. Levi lifts his right hand to shield his eyes from the sun and his vision zooms forward to a soldier perched up in the crow's nest of the ship, cranking an air raid siren in furious circles.

Levi looks away from the sea and down to the glass globe resting in his left hand. The ball of magnified glass reveals a domed scene where snowflakes float over a gory mountaintop plugged with miniature cabins. And all around the tiny wood cabins, even tinier figurines of broken people lie dead, strewn about in the snow in rigor mortis, their mouths rusted shut by dried blood.

He drops the terrifying snow globe of death and stares back to the ocean. The soldier in the old ship's pole mounted wooden basket ceases winding the air raid siren and turns to face the shore. Levi meets the sailor's vacant eyes from across the afar. The soldier's pupils become blazing suns. The sapphire blue in Levi's eyes morphs into full moons. A warning passes between them as the soldier blinks and his eyes become turning Earths.

Levi rips himself from the Hawaiian dream's suction and sits up in bed, breathing calmly as he tries to discard the strange dream, his senses hazy in the dark. After a moment, he scoots out of bed, careful not to disturb Naomi who is still sleeping soundly, and walks to the window.

The calm eye of the snowstorm moves over the mountain. Allowing him to stare up into a night sky cascading with a kaleidoscope of color. Bands of light arc and glide from a new solar flare hitting the eastern seaboard of the United States with the harbinger of electric death.

Naomi stirs behind him and mumbles something in her sleep before rolling over and tucking her head into the pillows. Levi watches her for a moment before turning back to the window. He stares up at the flaring Aurora Terra's lassos of aqua green, scarlet and violet light whipping through the atmosphere, wondering if the phenomenon's arrival in the night sky could be the rainbow described in the days of Noah after the Flood.

Down the hill, the mercenaries drop into the snow and look around at each other, wild eyed with the onslaught of alarming noise. Two try to rush the mound and are gunned down. Popped grenades burst in their hands and launch their broken bodies into the air as if they stepped on a land mine.

Clay Donegal motions for his troops to press forward and spread out. Their guns swallow bullets as they concentrate their fire on the bellowing nest. The sand bag beehive lights up with strafing gunfire as two more mercenaries run forward and lob two grenades onto the roof that pops the nest apart in a flash as the blaring siren and guard die in the howling wind.

Coffin Man's standing Erebus force of eighty five encircle the barracks, reload clips that gulp empty, and gun down five remaining guards in sprays of unrelenting gunfire. Then the assassins rush up the winding path to the lodge in a staggered line, their weapons swiveling side to side in search of more sentries.

The five remaining guards atop the hill spot engage the attacking force in a firefight from tree cover, chipping away a dozen more of Coffin Man's force before lethal bullets cut the last camp defenders down.

At the north gate, Outlander, Mallory, Bart and Clyde park the two vehicles and rest their blizzard strained eyes for a moment, as a bundled up National Guard soldier exits the entrance cabin and knocks on the sheriff's truck window. "Everything okay sir?"

"Yes," Outlander replies as he cracks the window. "Is everyone on post?"

"Yes, sir. We've got a platoon hunkered down in foxholes watching the road."

"Good. Let them know a convoy is coming. Keep the gate sealed until then."

"Are you still vacating the park in the morning?" the soldier asks.

"We're sticking to the plan. Proceed with the sweep after we leave."

"Will do, sir." The guard starts to turn away, "How about I bring you guys some coffee while you wait?"

"That would be good. Thank you, soldier." Outlander watches snow accumulate on the windshield faster than the wipers can remove it.

A half hour later, headlight beams penetrate the whiteout as a line of black SUVs appear from out of the storm. Outlander opens the glove compartment, removes a flare gun and opens his door. He steps out and fires an orange shot high over the northern entrance.

On the other side, a man climbs out from the middle of the line and trudges forward. He reaches Outlander's pickup truck and hops in the back seat. Shards of snow hang on Thorpe's cropped hair and a single flake melts in the crevice of a scar on his lip.

"Thorpe Cuyahoga, this is Mallory." They nod to each other as Outlander continues, "What kept you?"

"The roads. They're clogged. Debris and refugees everywhere. Slow goin'. Lot of pain out there. Hard on the eyes and heavy on the heart."

"I can only imagine. But will see for sure tomorrow when we move out. Do you have any wounded?" Outlander asks. "Got a medic in the vehicle behind us."

"Nah," Thorpe replies. "Just a lot of tired people itchin' for a few hours of rest."

"Any vehicles need fixin'? Got a mechanic here, too."

"Good to go on that front too once we refuel at camp." Thorpe shakes his head. "I just want us to be on our way and away from the vicinity of the Beltway. There are strange forces moving out there in the dark."

"Well, it will take a couple of hours to reach camp," the sheriff of Shenandoah warns as he wipes the fogged over windshield with the sleeve of his jacket so that he can see out into the night and maintain a line of sight with the idle convoy. "Break out the caffeine and follow us in and up."

Thorpe opens the backseat door and climbs out into the cold snowy wind. "See you up top."

Up at the lodge, Coffin Man's team breaches the now defenseless threshold of the camp and disperses along the ring of east side cabins. They unleash their weapons upon the sleeping Secret Eden tribes of Acadia and Congaree. Death knocks on lodge doors and operatives fall cabin by cabin like sleeping dominoes with divots punched all the way through.

Levi stands at his cabin window and watches the chopping wind pick up. A milky curtain of snowflakes blots out the night sky. Hypnotic flashes of zigzagging lightning flicker like a strobe, reaching into the crevices of the cabin before retracting back into the storm. His eyes widen with panic as he watches a line of grey shadows crest the mountaintop and move across the parking lot under the cover of the snowstorm. Stunned with horror, it takes a moment before he can decipher between night and nightmare. Then with another flash of phosphorescence, the danger is clear. He steels himself in the lightless room as shapes move about in the illuminated courtyard like ghosts climbing out of a grave.

Levi darts to the bed and rushes to get dressed. "Naomi, wake up!" He shakes her. "Hurry. Something's wrong. Terribly wrong. We need to get up and get ready." His chest tightens and he runs a worried hand through his long hair to try and calm his nerves.

Naomi sits up in bed alarmed. "What's the matter?"

"We're under attack. And they're coming," Levi says in a low growl as he fastens on his bulletproof vest.

"What?" she says in disbelief. "Who's attacking us? How?"

"I don't know," Levi says as he grabs his weapon. "Listen carefully, you need to get dressed now. If we don't fight back, we will die."

Naomi leaps out of bed and starts throwing on clothes. Then grips her weapons beside Levi as they stand at the desk and watch gunfire rip the east side of lodge complex. "Could this be a drill?"

"No way. Just watch." He tries to swallow his racing thoughts but chokes and splashes them across his mind's eye. Worry floods his rattled veins. Nausea rips at his gut. Ambient terror gathers. He breathes rapidly, trying to slow his pulse, pushing air deep into his lungs until they fill in protest. Grave concern seared into his eyes. "You'll see." He reaches for and holds Naomi's hand.

Fully armed death commandos cross the field of snow and close in on the west side of camp. Naomi lets go of Levi's hand

and places her palm across her mouth as she concentrates on the unfolding nightmare.

"We're socked in by the weather." He looks over at her and sees flashes of lightening reflect out of Naomi's eyes. "We could make it to my truck a few feet away but we'd still have to drive through that."

"There's no time. We wouldn't make it far." She looks around the room. "The mattress won't shield us." She motions to the closet. "There. That'll have to do."

They move into the cramped closet and aim their guns at the cabin door. Naomi steals a quick glance to her side and meets Levi's eyes. "This is bad."

"It's beyond that," he says as he clicks his loaded M4 machine gun's safety off and crouches in the closet, waiting for the danger roaming out in the night to arrive at their doorstep.

Rapid breathes from flowing anxiety fill the tense silence of the closet. They try to steady their hands for the coming fight. Seconds pass. Two dark objects burst through the windows and land on the bed. Levi seizes the closet door and yanks it shut. A violent concussion shakes the small enclosure and brightness penetrates the door's wooden cracks. Cold seeping air burrows under the door as a volley of bullets spray the room. They hear bullets thumping the wood walls like knuckles of lead as he cracks a slit in the closet door to risk a glance.

The cabin door rips off its hinges and slams awkwardly against the wall. Two figures in Arctic snow suits rush in with their weapons raised. Levi and Naomi fire their weapons from their defensive position. The first man erupts in a dark mist as their bullets punch him back into the wall and he slides to the floor. The second man takes a direct shot to the head and crumples in the doorway.

"They'll keep coming," he whispers. "We need to find an escape route."

"Not yet," she says, "There's too many of them still out there."

"My truck is parked right beside the cabin," Levi says. "It may be concealed under a layer of snow by now. We could try and shelter in the back of it until daylight."

They start to move but fresh hail of gunfire flies into the room, pock marking the back wall. Another assassin bursts up the steps. Levi and Naomi shoot and knock the man down on the porch, his body twitching as erupting wounds pin him to the ground. They continue firing until a bullet grazes the chin and uncorks the neck. A rush of blood spills as they cease fire and the assassin's head rolls to the side and falls still. They stare in shock at the brutality of the combat and fold back into the closet.

Levi ejects his spent magazine and loads fresh ammo. "Are you hit?"

"No. I'm okay," anguish in her voice.

Lightning flashes outside. The room lights up briefly as they nod to one another with resolve before easing out of the closet to try and make a run for the truck outside. Slow seconds pass as they approach the open doorway. A new attack from an unseen shooter sends a spray of bullets into the room. Metal slugs rip through the bed like searching fists as stray rounds pound the furniture and back wall. They drop to the floor and return aimless fire into the night as they crawl backwards to the closet.

"We're trapped," Naomi whispers. "I don't want to die like this."

"Me either."

A running shape approaches to the cabin and bounds the steps. Naomi and Levi fire from their nook in the corner. Impacting bullets pinball the shape around in the doorway until it skids to a stop by the desk and writhes into a stone death grip.

While Levi and Naomi reload in the darkness, a silver circle is lobbed into the cabin from an unseen hand out in the night. Naomi yanks Levi back towards the closet as the object tumbles through the air. They pivot and dive as the stun grenade detonates and the room explodes in bright flashing light. The last painful image Levi sees is Naomi lying unconscious on the ground beside him.

An hour later, atop the mountain, Levi wakes up in the lodge's den facing a fire dancing in the hearth. Sore from the stun grenade's punch, he takes a sharp breath as he struggles to orient himself. A faint ringing sound occupies his ears. Blood bubbles out of his busted nose. He chokes on a separate stream of metallic tasting fluid running down his throat. He coughs and lurches forward only to be halted by bound wrists. And then he realizes the danger has not passed.

Outside, the blizzard presses on the lodge as if trying to shake the structure loose. Levi scoots up to a sitting position. The air is cold, but the fire and his thick pea coat keep him warm. He struggles with the metal handcuffs hooked around a wrought iron table that once held magazines and the propped feet of travelers.

Then he looks over and sees Naomi in unconscious captivity on the opposite corner of the long table. He rips at the handcuffs with fury until the skin along his wrists tears and his shoulders go numb. His mind screams, and he clamps his jaw to hold back a primal roar of anguish. He squeezes his eyes shut in sorrow. Then a dormant survival instinct surfaces from a place that he ventured to during his lost year. He quiets his mind and begins breathing exercises, focusing all attention on the forced breaths flowing in and out. In and out until a small measure of calm eases his nerves and the fear reluctantly fades into a state of heightened awareness where slow seconds pass. He resolves to face these final moments with some semblance of dignity for all the wonderful things he experienced in his journey here to this mortal moment.

Out in the lobby, boots clomp in cadence along the wooden floor. Beside him, Naomi comes wide awake with a loud wail which fades to a moan before her head sags down and her beautiful chin meets the top of her bulletproof vest. Levi swivels back and forth from Naomi to the approaching sound as tall shadows climb along the wall from the hearth's wicking flames.

A line of men in chalk arctic suits enters the room. They all look the same with their black load bearing units strapped on and concrete colored wind masks concealing their faces. A sinister circle of surviving assassins forms around Levi and Naomi. Then their masked faces turn to a leader. Levi can hear him walking the back perimeter of the den. The sounds of his feet come closer and he leaps up on the table. Its thick slab of wood absorbs the weight with a slight vibration.

Levi eyelids fall down, and he rests for a moment. Until he feels the unseen man's breath against his neck. He stays inside his head, not yet wanting to venture back out. Fear pulses into the pit of an empty stomach. He feels burning vomit force its way up his throat. He leans sideways and ejects the acrid liquid as a foamy splatter across the wooden floor, imagining it is surf brushing over the side of an old ship roaming free along the surface of a vast ocean.

The man behind Levi laughs contempt and the flanking minions follow. The more the men laugh and taunt, the more Levi is glad to have fought back and taken a piece of evil down with his fallen tribe. He refuses to let the men kill his spirit if he is in the final moments of his life.

Naomi comes awake again and calls for Levi in a den of captivity.

"I'm here. Sshhh." As Levi turns to her, the man perched on the table collides a painful punch that causes Levi's head to swing left and roll back to center.

"My name is Coffin Man. Stay awake, boy." He grabs Levi's scalp and bends it back. "The tribes of Acadia and Congaree are no more. We destroyed them." Coffin Man squeezes Levi's cheeks and forces the eyes to face him as he dangles a bear's severed head. "*Ursus Americanus.* A trophy."

Levi is completely unprepared for the lifeless image staring back and dry heaves. Coffin Man takes pleasure from the effect of the talisman in his hands and shoves Levi's head away from his grasp. Then he hops down off the table and walks towards the fire. His other hand carries a second smaller bear skull in its grasp. The men part as their leader tosses the bear heads into the fire.

Flame devours the black blood matted fur. The tissue on the bears' faces melts away until two helmets of bone sit atop the fire with clamped jaws filled with primal knives. Empty eye sockets loom over large hollow nostrils as the stench of singed fur and flesh creeps through the room.

Coffin Man walks from the fireplace looking like a mohawked lunatic giant and unsheathes a blade. The waking nightmare continues. "You don't recognize me yet but we bumped into each other a couple of weeks back." He smiles. "You two are two lucky. We could've just as easily put a double tap into each of your skulls. After all, you killed some of our friends. Instead we dragged you up here so we could play."

Levi's imagination becomes haunted by what this man can do to him while he is chained to the table. Coffin Man places the cold knife against the skin of Levi's face. The Shenandoah operative closes his eyes and grits his teeth as the blade slices into his left cheek and tears a slanted slit. Levi feels a warm curtain of blood slide out. Its crimson line breaks and drops liquid beads onto his navy coat. Levi shakes with fury against the handcuffs that bind him in place.

"To mark you," Coffin Man says as he rises and walks to Naomi.

Levi screams at him to stop. Naomi looks over at him and shakes her head. Then she spits on Coffin Man as he draws close.

Coffin Man unleashes a vicious slap across Naomi's face. Then he turns to Levi. "Shall I gut your girl like a piece of trout in one of those streams running down the mountain?" Levi locks his jaw in horror. "She's got spunk. I'm curious to see how long she can flop around with her entrails dragging the floorboards before she bleeds out."

Levi shakes his head slowly with pleading eyes. Coffin Man's cold mask looks away and refocuses on his toy. He cups Naomi's chin in his hand. Blood trickles from her lip and down across the fingers of his glove as he makes an incision across Naomi's right cheek and pushes her face out of his palm. "And to mark you."

Outside the den's broad windows, the intensity of the snowstorm pauses, sheets of snow come in smaller waves and the wind changes its howl to a whistle as if the storm does not want to obstruct its view of the torture. Coffin Man lifts his wind mask to reveal yet another mask of skeletal black and white face paint punctuated with cold blinking eyes. He wipes their blood from the blade before sheathing it and motioning his assassins forward. The room shrinks inward. The noose tightens until the attackers swarm Levi's view.

"Where are the sheriffs Outlander Shenandoah and Thorpe Cuyahoga?"

"I don't know," Levi answers in confusion. He assumed that Outlander had already been hit in the attack.

"How about I peel back your scalp and run a cheese grater over your brain?" Coffin Man threatens. "Would that help your memory?"

"You lost them didn't you?" Naomi taunts to distract their attention.

Coffin Man points a gloved finger down at her. "Maybe not, we killed so many of you it's hard to tell who's who. So wipe that smirk off your face."

Naomi's smile fades into hate filled resolve at his chilling words as she stares up at Coffin Man and focuses on not blinking.

"The only reason you two are still alive is so that you can deliver a message to them when they return to camp. I want them to know that they have a choice. Stop leading the eastern tribes west and find somewhere quiet to live out your lives. Or press on and all of you will die. One of you will repeat it and the other one will confirm it. That's all you have to do."

Naomi and Levi say nothing as they sit chained to the table with blood running down their cheeks.

"Tell the sheriffs of Shenandoah and Cuyahoga that the Potomac Guard are hunting Defcon Denver. Tell them we will kill the rest of Secret Eden at the rendezvous in Yellowstone National Park." Coffin Man repeats the message and demands that Naomi and Levi recite it back to him. "Secret Eden is doomed. So when the two sheriffs return, tell them what I am telling you now." Then the room empties and the invaders fade away.

Fatigue pulls Levi down. Saltwater tears well in Naomi's jade eyes as she begins to sing to him in a soft mournful voice. "*The whole world is a narrow bridge. But what matters most is to not be afraid.*" She repeats the Jewish hymn with the tone of a lullaby, her voice flowing like a mockingbird's song until she is hoarse.

They fall asleep captive as the fire's flames turn the bark to ash and the logs crumble into chunks of burning amber. Their warmth burns away into the cold deadly night.

The snowstorm gradually passes, the light of a new day comes into the sky, and they wake to sounds of feet running across wooden floorboards.

Outlander and Mallory enter the den with guns at the ready and rage plastered across their faces.

"We thought you were dead," Naomi says with wide eyes. "How did you survive? It was a bloodbath. Where were you?"

"I'm so sorry." Outlander shoulders his weapon as he begins to work to free her from the numbing grip of the cuffs. "At the north gate meeting the Cuyahoga team. They were delayed.

Then it took longer to make it back. Trees were cut to block the road and slow us down."

"How bad is it out there?" Levi asks Mallory as she works on his cuffs with a multi tool.

"Dozens of dead are strewn around the mountain top. Jody is gone," Mallory says. "And most of the vehicles stolen. Hold still."

"We killed some," Naomi mumbles through blue lips as Outlander releases her shackles. "But there were too many. They tore through here."

"They breached the camp under the cover of the snowstorm and started killing," Levi says as Mallory unlocks his cuffs and helps him up into a rocking chair. He squeezes fists and then stretches his fingers in full extension, repeating the process to help get the circulation flowing.

"Who did this?" Outlander asks through steaming breath and hinged anger. "And why did they let you live?"

"To tell you this," Naomi relays Coffin Man's message and warning as she rubs the black and blue ligature marks on her wrists.

"Operatives were not supposed to know about Yellowstone until we reach the Badlands." Outlander's face reddens with anger. "Now it's a race."

A platoon of Cuyahoga men and women enter the lobby, and remain back at a respectful distance to the Shenandoah survivors.

Mallory points to a stranger, "That's Thorpe."

"They were looking for him too," Naomi says.

Thorpe steps forward, "The attackers lifted the bulletproof vests with entry patches from the chests of the dead. They can use them like stolen keys to gain entry to the various check points along the road ahead."

"We have to keep moving," Outlander says. "We all saw that solar flare last night. The capital zone is as dangerous as ever. Thorpe, do you have any intel?"

"It's hard to say. Only murmurs and rumors," he says. "There was some talk along the Beltway about a legion of paramilitary mercenaries mixed in with other fighters recruited as cannon fodder from gangs or straight out of situations of sheer desperation."

"For what aim?" Mallory asks.

Thorpe shakes his head, "Don't know for sure yet. Best guess is the fallback sites in Colorado are about to be targeted. And they're hollowing out elements of the plan along the way."

"Are you referring to Defcon Denver?" Naomi asks.

"Yes," Thorpe replies. "The coastal cities are too vulnerable now. The federal government is uniting in Boulder, Denver, Colorado Springs, and Pueblo."

Outlander places a stack of fresh logs in the fireplace and pops a flare to get them going. Mallory returns from the kitchen and hands Naomi and Levi wet cloths to clean up with as Bart and Clyde enter.

"Perimeter has been secured. The National Guard platoon from the north gate are helping identify the dead," Bart says to Outlander and then stops. "Levi and Naomi, gotta say, it's a nice surprise seeing you two alive on such a dark day."

"You too," Levi says.

"Your truck is undamaged," Bart says. "Resting under a layer of snow beside your busted cabin. The snow concealed it. They didn't see it. How bout I pull it around for you?"

"That'd be good. Keys are in my backpack in my room," Levi breathes a sigh of relief and stares through the den windows and out over rolling snow covered hills. "Thanks, man."

"Bart, can you please grab my gear too from Levi's room and load it?" Naomi asks.

"Sure thing," Bart says as he exits the den.

Clyde stoops beside Levi and Naomi and pops open his

medic kit while he examines them. "We need to sew you two up and get you road ready," he says, "Do you need a painkiller while I stitch up your cheeks?"

"No," Levi shakes his head. "It'll fog my head. A couple of aspirin will do."

"I'll take his," Naomi quips.

They share a faint smile as Clyde passes a painkiller to Naomi and opens the medical kit to thread a needle. "Your cheeks should heal over time," Clyde says as he pushes back Naomi's bangs and places a hand on her forehead feeling for signs of fever before he starts to repair her cheek by digging loops of stitching into the wound to tug the skin back into place. Then he moves to Levi.

Afterwards, Naomi struggles to her feet and presses a bandage tight against her cheek. She wraps a blanket around her shoulders and walks to the den windows, looking out over a calm landscape that seems in such contrast to the night before.

"We need to be on the road heading west," Outlander says he puts a plug of tobacco chew in his cheek. "Let's load up and move out."

Outside, the snow glistens and Levi feels the warm sun warm on his face while he breathes in the crisp mountain air. Bart pulls Levi's truck up the hill and parks it beside his SUV, hops out and tosses Levi the keys as sweeper vehicles carrying grimacing National Guard soldiers push up the hill and into the lodge parking lot.

Outlander walks to meet them. "There's death all over the place and the ground's too hard to dig graves by hand," motioning to the ring of scorched cabins. "Leave part of your team behind to take Secret Eden's dead down to the barracks and give them a proper burial inside. Then seal the building. The visitor center is now a tomb."

"Sir, what do you want us to do with the rest of the dead?" the sergeant who gave him the coffee last night asks.

Outlander looks around and spots a few invader corpses laying about, half covered by snow. "Drag 'em up here to the parking lot, douse the pile in gasoline, and burn 'em in a pyre." He spits a stream of brown tobacco juice and walks to the flag pole in the center of the parking lot. Outlander unfastens the rope, lowers the American flag, and unhooks it. Then he takes the flag to the back roll bar of his pickup truck and ties it on.

The Shenandoah survivors climb into their vehicles and drive out of the Skyland Lodge parking lot. Levi follow's Outlander and Mallory's silver pickup, with Naomi sitting in the shotgun seat beside him, and watches the wind catch the red, white and blue fabric of the flag as the convoy descends the hill and turns right on Skyline Drive. They travel the road south and follow the depression of tire tracks in the deep snow that the attackers carved hours earlier. An icy fog rolls over the hills, making it seem as if they are driving through the clouds.

At Waynesboro, Virginia they pass through a defeated checkpoint at the entrance to the Blue Ridge Parkway. Bullet riddled bodies of National Guard soldiers pepper the snowy site. With no time to provide decent burial they clear booby traps in the road and drive on, remaining within a boundary of the national park system that no longer feels safe despite the calm scenery of snow covered mountain ridges staring in from the windows. The small caravan travels along the long empty road of the parkway, past miles of stacked stone guard rails hooked with rampart overlooks.

Naomi looks over at Levi, "That giant told us they were going to Yellowstone to bait us. They want to deplete us into irrelevance."

He nods and fixes tired eyes on the spellbinding road ahead.

BLUE RIDGE
PARKWAY

Day 21

The convoy drives the remaining road of the parkway and passes into Smoky Mountains National Park, a refuge that contains more varieties of tree species than the entire continent of Europe. The vehicles veer off the road at Black Gap and navigate a forest labyrinth of soggy dirt roads until reaching a dead end holding a long line of vehicles from the Everglades, Biscayne, Virgiland, and Smoky tribes. The National Guard vehicles pull up short and wait as the Shenandoah survivors drive forward with the Cuyahoga team, park and climb out of their trucks.

"Thorpe. Outlander." A woman with braided hair, purple face paint, and yellow circles tracking up her cheeks says as she scans the convoy. "Where is the rest of your team?" her breath puffing a small cloud of steam.

"It's just us, Shaconage," Outlander says as he removes his cowboy hat and wipes at fatigue. "Shenandoah was attacked last night. Congaree and Acadia were wiped out."

"How?" the sheriff of the Smoky tribe asks in a deadly whisper.

"I was out the north gate meeting Thorpe. They were

delayed." Outlander shakes his head as he pulls out a tobacco pouch and inserts a fresh plug of chew. "The camp was attacked from the east. Through the trial system by a militia aiming for Yellowstone and then Denver. We need to be on the road headin' west. And quickly. They stole Secret Eden vests from the dead."

"Then let's get going," Shaconage says as she processes the implications. "You look like you've been up all night, Outlander. I'll drive your truck so you can brief me and then rest up. Same for the drivers in rest of your force."

Soon the six merged tribes form a long line and wind down a steep mountain pass. They navigate a terrain of switchbacks as the caravan trudges over Newfound Gap and across the Appalachian Trail, the road eventually carrying them down into the pioneer homesteads of Cade's Cove.

The roughly two hundred men and women, and seventy vehicles, reach the eerie and silent town of Gatlinburg at sunset. Tacky trinket shops and garish museums with dormant neon lights shuttered along main street. Remnants of the sacrifice of a beautiful town to commercialism. They follow flowing mountain streams through the Cherokee National Forest and past dark cabins with sparking circuit boxes. They move through the land, certain that the mountain community's distrustful eyes are undoubtedly upon them as the mechanized line passes by. An occasional shift of a curtain the only sign of life.

"I have kin near here," Levi says to Naomi in the back seat as a Biscayne operative drives. "These hills are full of hollows, sparsely populated by strong people, who are not afraid to take up arms to defend one another. I don't know about our coasts and borders, but Appalachia is invasion proof."

In the early evening they roll through Knoxville, a town that is barely recognizable. A lone riot police squad is out on patrol below an overpass. Abandoned office towers stalk them as they drive I-40 due west, heading towards a connect to the Eisenhower

Interstate System and its network of rest stop bivouac sites. Secret Eden's surviving Shenandoah team adapting to the realization that they are no longer tucked away on rural land as they aim for survival on a vulnerable urban road of ruin.

The scene is the same in Nashville, just on a larger scale. Clogged necropolis roads sprawl out from the depopulating city that has been unplugged from the Information Age. Levi recalls a young soldier's blank stare and burned out words at a rest stop as they smoked a cigarette while staring out over an eighteen wheeler junkyard.

"The cities are dying," the kid had said while the eastern tribes replenished their supplies. "I see their refugees every day. There's too much desperation along the road."

MEMPHIS

Day 22

A lead team of tactical vehicles deposits the caravan off I-40 in the jugular of Memphis where staccato bursts of gunfire rake the alleys of the Blues City as afternoon fades into evening. They roll through the tall tree lined parkways of Midtown and pass by a college campus with Gothic architecture where blocks of quarried limestone and sandstone rise to roofs layered in tiles of blue shale. The convoy cuts through wide empty streets strewn with debris and shards of glass as they move deeper into the maze, past abandoned storefronts among a confetti of ruin, turn west and drive along River Street where the Memphis Pyramid cuts into the skyline. Two miles later they reach a park on a bluff overlooking the Mississippi River that has been converted into a fort. Cargo container walls and sandbag perches manned by sentries run the perimeter of the bivouac site.

The gates open and a sheriff with camouflage face paint, a shaved scalp and wearing Hot Springs insignia walks out with a squad of guards in tow.

Outlander approaches the entrance with Shaconage and Thorpe. "How long before we can be on the move?" he asks.

"The rest of the eastern tribes are all here. I'm holding two for us over there." Youngblood points across the pallet scattered grounds to a pair of coal burning trains sitting idle on oxidized steel tracks that lead across the state line to Arkansas. "Trains have been passing through about every hour. A lot of supplies and people on the move. We can squeeze in the middle of the schedule. How does thirty minutes sound? We can use the time to load the vehicles onto the flatcars, tie 'em down and secure the bulkheads."

"I'll spread the word," Outlander says. "And then I need to brief you on some developments."

A half hour later, a shrill whistle blows as the lead locomotive rolls slowly across the bridge high above the Mississippi River, carrying a hundred and fifty members of the Mammoth, Smoky, Virgiland and Biscayne tribes. When it reaches the other side of the bridge, it picks up speed and heads towards the Arkansas horizon. A second locomotive follows minutes later, carrying a combined force of another one hundred and fifty from the Tortugas, Everglades, Hot Springs, Cuyahoga parks, plus six surviving members of the Shenandoah tribe.

The pair of trains move out of Memphis, splitting the distance like steel syringes aimed at a vein of uncertainty in the long dark scar of the cities beyond. Fresh scenery overlays the images from the final night in Shenandoah. Naomi stays close to Levi and they keep their faces turned towards the open fields rushing by outside their window. Levi is a mess, but so is the world. For the first time in a long time, he has something in common with the mainstream.

Time drifts by as Southern scenery melts away along the countryside through vast stretches of territory. Arkansas, Missouri and Kansas pass by in increments. The land morphs into desolate prairie and the trains arc into the heartland. Levi and Naomi catch up on rest, each of them waking startled at times from haunting dystopian dreams as the trains travel deep into the interior.

The track delivers the eastern tribes to North Platte, Nebraska where grain silos bunch together in towering concrete six packs beside old pioneer trails and a thin river. The steel ribbon widens into the jaws of the Union Bailey Yard, the nation's largest railroad classification depot, where two dozen paths spread out from a steel compass as the industrial line rolls to a stop along a massive grid surrounded by corn fields. Hundreds of wheeled containers towing cargo of coal, fuel, stockyard livestock, grain, and assorted supplies are queued up and wearing intermittent tags of spray paint graffiti, waiting to be led by tough bumblebee colored engines steered by denim overalled conductors.

THE
BADLANDS

Day 23

'Wake up, honey." Naomi touches Levi's cheek. "It's your watch." Her words and the smell of hot coffee penetrate the haze of a restless sleep.

He wakes to a passenger car full of cold stale air. Levi accepts the cup and takes sips while Naomi tends to his facial wound and sets fresh bandages. Then he sifts through a pile of gear in the seat beside him. He slips on his cowboy boots and clips his pistol into a slot on his bulletproof vest. He slides an arm through each loop of the armor and adjusts the straps until the fit is snug. The yellow and black Secret Eden patch over his heart containing the warning color pattern of nature's stinging insects. Levi stands, tugs a wool cap down over his ears, sets wind goggles on the front of the cap just above his forehead, and wraps a scarf around his neck. Then he puts on the thick pea coat.

Naomi lies back on the seats across the aisle. "Where will you go when this is all over?"

Levi looks out the window into the passing fields of the Dakotalands where long stretches of wheat, barley, rye and sorghum vie for dominance among encroaching grass.

"Home to Alabama."

She props herself up on her elbows. "Would I like it there?"

"Southern life is subtle. Like a well-kept secret." Levi stands and nods. "You could be happy there."

"I would like to find a secluded place on a beach where we can shut out the world and listen to the ocean touch the shore." Naomi lays back and closes her eyes for a moment. "We could live in a hut surrounded by palm trees. With a porch where the breeze passes by at sunset. And a catamaran pulled up onto the sand. I wish that can be our life," she pouts and opens her green eyes that hold a tinge of sadness, "But we're a long way from the beach."

"We are, but certain dreams are worth holding onto." Levi shoulders his machine gun and winks at her as he slides on a pair of gloves. "I'll see you in a little while." He steps along the center gangway to the back of the train and pauses at a window to watch morning sun rays paint the rolling prairie a hundred hues of yellow.

When he slides the back door open, cold autumn wind slaps him awake as he steps onto a small balcony and pushes the door closed. A blur of gravel and steel track rush by the mesh grating under his feet. Levi looks left to the north flank's machine gun turret and nods to a gunner who is perched on a stagecoach seat with dreadlocks flapping in the deflected wind.

"Mornin'," the man calls in a Cajun accent straight from the cypress and moss swamps of rural Louisiana. "Sheriff Zulu Everglades."

"Levi Shenandoah."

Zulu pops in a piece of chewing gum and surveys the sky and the rain clouds gathering in it.

Levi leans against the balcony's welded metal wall and glances over at an empty nest and a massive gun barrel with its nose pointing down as if taking a nap. "What'd they cobble this little fortress together from?"

"Beale Street horse buggies and Mississippi River mud packed into burlap sacks," Zulu says as he kicks the sandbags and knocks a fist against a sturdy windshield. "The riot shields were strung together with piano wire from a looted music warehouse near the bluff. And there is an inch thick plate of steel between the sandbags."

The rush of cold air relents as Levi climbs up on a narrow stagecoach bench and settles into the turret facing the southern flank, listening to the wind whistling through the cracks.

"I caught your accent," Zulu says. "You missin' SEC football as much as I am about now?"

"Sure am." Levi props his feet on the sandbags and rests his elbows on cracked leather padding. "Back during the yester days I woulda been looking forward to the upcoming Iron Bowl. Grilling out with friends and family, drinking some beer and rootin' for the Tide against the Tigers." He grips the handles of a hulking M61 Vulcan Gatling gun and scans the stretch of streaming land for signs of danger. "But it seems like those days passed by miles ago." Levi's eyes strain under the languid spell of the frontier. "You know where we are?"

"I'll look for a marker." Zulu Everglades grabs a pair of binoculars from a cargo pocket. "You see anything on your side?"

"Only the occasional dilapidated red barn."

A few minutes later, Zulu spots what he is looking for and calls over his shoulder. "We're inbound."

"How close?"

"Real close. Come on, I'll show you." Zulu points over the prairie where a road starts to run parallel to the train tracks. "That's I-90 West. The number on the exit sign tells how far we are from the Wyoming state line. We've got about another hour left."

The two trains roll through the outskirts of desolate Kadoka, South Dakota. Dark billowing clouds from an approaching storm blot out the blue sky. Gusts of moisture laden wind blow across the prairie, pressing down on a golden sea of prairie cordgrass and bluestem. Levi and Zulu continue to scan fields of crops and rangeland that spreads as far as the eye can see. Many of the stalks are snapped in half, as if the only way to survive is to bend and sway to more powerful forces.

A sign flashes by welcoming them to the Buffalo Gap National Grassland. Diverse patches of prairie intertwine. Indian grass weaving with canary grass and wild rye. Another sign rushes by for the Cactus Flat at Exit 131 five miles ahead. In the distance, a herd of wild buffalo roam as the jagged buttes of Badlands National Park spear up from the edge of the falling horizon like the mouth of a shark. The buffalo pound the black earth as they turn from the chugging train and stampede through the switchgrass, heading deep into the prairie.

Up ahead, Sheriff Shaconage stands beside the conductor on the lead train's engine car and stares out the cab front window, watching the tracks flow through a golden field and curve into a straightaway that will run them the last few miles to their destination. Seconds later she gasps as a flood of panic squirts through her veins. Shaconage shoots an arm up to the handle of the warning horn. Screeching decibels shatter the cold tranquility of America's largest ecosystem, blaring a signal of imminent danger.

Dozens of moving scarecrows fall back into the tallgrass as they tug ropes tied to the parallel steel rails and open them up like a zipper. Slats peel away from the center of the track and roll in opposites directions into the prairie as if the hammered binding spikes have turned to rust dust. The stunned conductor and sheriff watch severed pieces of the railroad flatten the grass in horizontal lines on both sides of the track as they are dragged away. The absence creating an ambush road of gravel along ladder rungs of rickety railroad ties.

The tailing train hears the horn and locks its brakes down onto the tracks. Sparks shoot from the wheels like bursting fireworks.

The lead train leaves the safety of the tracks, grinds its steel wheels across empty yards of railroad ties and gravel, and misses the connect to the bending prongs where the curving tracks resume. The derailing mass of inertia carries the Biscayne, Mammoth, Smoky and Virgiland tribes in a straight line into the prairie. The engine car dips into a sickening lean, tips the adjoining cars, and pulls a derailing ripple effect the through aimless transport. Car after car curves into the field, colliding with solid ground, rolling into somersaults, and blasting up black dirt as if they are impacting meteorites. The land trembles. Crumpling metal screams as it squeezes life from the broken passengers like an accordion of death. Then the pummeled train goes still and releases lines of fire that spread through the damaged compartments and over any surviving passengers.

"Lock and load," the Everglades sheriff calls from his turret, "And chew 'em up."

Levi and Zulu swivel their Vulcan gun barrels and aim into the fields as momentum propels them towards the metal inferno up ahead. They tighten their grips on the Gatling guns and breath as they hook index fingers around the triggers. Then their fingers pull gun mounted ripcords that unleash heavy strafing runs of defensive tracer fire into the prairie as scarecrows with painted faces rise from the field in camouflage ghillie suits as devastating bullets rip them from their hiding spots. They dash and scatter in terrain blending garb.

Levi leans into the jackhammer recoils. Strips of blazing bullets feed through the barrel that chews as it wags side to side in raking sweeps. Large caliber slugs tear into enemy torsos and toss fistfuls of blood into the cold air as smoking spent bullet casings bounce around inside the nest and sear his uniform as they nick like brass thorns.

The defensive aim of heavy bullets from the train balcony gun turrets joust with scarecrows that rise out of the swaying golden prairie grass. A swell of orange muzzles flash through the field. Bullets careen at the train, whacking against the metal sides and stabbing into turret sandbags. The jigsaw of riot shields spider web as Levi and Zulu rip return fire into the grassland until the gun barrels spin empty.

Levi quickly pops a fresh canister and threads a new chain into Gatling jaws. All along the remaining train's passenger cars, side windows yank down, operatives aim, and machine guns return fire. Gun smoke hovers and blurs the view. The surviving train's speed drops, but the distance to the molten pyre of wreckage ahead is not shrinking fast enough. Zulu and Levi brace themselves as they continue to fire into the fields.

Impact. The slowing surviving train collides with a sideways caboose from the dismembered lead train. Tremors of trauma shake the cars all the way back to the tail section.

When the aftershocks fade, the eastern operatives resume unleashing guttural bursts of gunfire into the field. Muzzle blasts and speeding metal slugs chip away at fighters from both sides. Scarecrows stagger around with wounds and fall to the ground. Holes pock mark the train cars as moans from the wounded bloom. Chaotic seconds pass. Muzzles aims wildly and spread arcs of fire into the tallgrass. The bottled up operatives begin to flee the confines of the passengers cars and gain new cover as they disperse and crawl under the halted train's undercarriage, using the heavy steel to buffer the enveloping attack. But ricocheting bullets pinball away any semblance of safety.

The stark swaying terrain of the Badlands offers the shrinking tribes no sanctuary from the ambush as their enemy, still a hundred strong, digs in and surrounds them from the north and south flanks.

Wind rises along with the battle and its constant press causes

Levi's jaw to clench as he braces against the cold. Fear knots his chest as he struggles to take a full deep breath inside a halo of combat anxiety. Levi and Zulu's red hot gun barrels spin empty a second time. They unsling their M4 machine guns, rock back the slides and hop down from their stagecoach seats as dark clouds and thunderheads close in and toss hard pellets of sleet and frigid rain down on the prairie.

The scarecrows fade farther back into the sea of golden grass and vanish under the cover of poisonous black smoke pouring out of the destroyed lead train. Thorpe and Naomi emerge onto the balcony as the surviving Tortugas, Everglades, Hot Springs, Cuyahoga and Shenandoah platoons fan out in defensive lines along the north and south sides of the railroad tracks and then rush into high grass with their guns blazing. A brutal shooting gallery manifests on the prairie as north and south lines of Secret Eden walk forward with chattering guns that scatter the scarecrows.

"Naomi, you're with me," Thorpe orders as he points to a ladder leading to the roof. "We'll lay down some cover fire from high ground."

Naomi locks eyes with Levi. Then lets go as she follows Thorpe up the ladder to the train's roof.

"I'll go north. You head south," Zulu says as he steps to the edge of the balcony like a coiled spring. He looks back at Levi with determined eyes wild with anger. "Watch your six and kill anything in your path." Then he leaps and disappears into the tallgrass, vanishing among the swaying reeds as he runs to join the battle.

Levi steps to the edge of the balcony and jumps down into soft earth, feeling his cowboy boots sink into the landing. He enters a sea of grass with his submachine gun level to the prairie's severed serenity and plows ahead into chest high bluestem grass in pursuit of the ghillie scarecrows. Sounds of the spreading battle reach his ears and the smell of wet grass blends with cordite. Spikelets whip by as his arms push through thickets of thin stalks as his boots mash the ground. Cold rain continues to pour out of the Dakota sky. Levi wipes moisture from his eyes with the sleeve of his coat and finds no enemies as he moves a hundred yards out from the train.

He ducks and pulls his scarf around his mouth to choke off his steaming breath. Then he turns west and begins to walk slowly, listening and watching for flanking movement. The field sways in the wind. Sounds of gunfire and wounded cries dart up from the prairie as he continues moving in his sweep. Fire from the smoldering wreckage sizzles and curls in a widening cloud as gun battles erupt inside of Buffalo Gap National Grassland. Barrels blaze and it becomes impossible to distinguish the source of the hand held death as friend or foe. As the battle in the reeds rages, Levi slogs into the foray. He zigzags through the pathless maze of grass, rabid for his enemy.

Suddenly arching bullets whiz by in front of him and Levi hears voices ahead of him howl in anguish. A scarecrow rises, stumbles through the grass and dies. Levi spins back to the train and spots Naomi lying prone on the roof. She lifts a hand and motions for him to continue on before she swivels to face the other side of the tracks.

Levi tracks two ghillie suited scarecrows crawling across the ground, their fingers digging scorpion tail lines into the earth as they pull themselves forward with bullet wounds stitched up their legs and backs. He does not wait for any more details to register. The submachine gun in his hands rips a long burst. The grass shreds and a bloody mist sprays. Small streaks of fire burn the blonde stalks and quickly fizzle out to wisps of smoke.

He ejects the magazine and smacks a fresh one in as a scarecrow rises up over a patch of barley grass in the distance and shoots at him. Levi ducks under the bullets and grits his teeth in anger. He returns defensive fire from the cold wet ground until the second magazine empties and the odor of spent shells is thick in the air. He stoops low and moves around the target in an arc, spotting his wounded prey staggering away with a trail of red leaking from a neck wound. Levi loads another magazine, aims, and fires a three shot burst. He watches red globs erupt from between the scarecrow's shoulder blades as the man collapses.

Elsewhere, sporadic bursts of gunfire continue to pepper the prairie as he passes through swaying thin alleys of death with cautious eyes and an alert trigger. A surreal aloneness of the prairie envelops him while he tries to sense the danger roaming nearby. The crackle of gunfire trickles off and then fades entirely as the clashes go silent. Something shifts within the battlefield. Screams start riding the wind. The vibe becomes different. Less fluid, more patient. So he moves with nature and bends as it bends, sways as it sways, looking for unnatural movement.

An operative with a Cuyahoga patch runs by on his periphery and he eases off the trigger. Levi remains on the outskirts of the fight, looking for a route to cut in. It takes a few dozen more yards through a wall of neck high prairie cordgrass before a sign of conflict reappears fifty yards away. Clyde and a Hot Springs operative peek up from the field as the grass leans from a gust of air. Reeds and spikelets bounce against their cheeks as they sense something lurking nearby. Their submachine guns swivel, covering their movements. Horror punches Levi and he begins to run towards them.

Clyde and the woman beside him squeeze off random rounds into the ground around them. Fright carves deep into their faces as their mouths puff quick steaming breaths that send smoke signals to the enemy. A stealth scarecrow rises beside the woman and the assassin's arm whips out a flash of metal that slices through the air and glides through her neck. Her body topples. The scarecrow spins and catches the Clyde as he turns. A curved sling blade sinks into the medic's armpit. The scarecrow grins as he hears air deflate from Clyde's punctured lung. Clyde's face contorts in pain as his gun is ripped from his rigid hands and a second blade slices across his lower stomach in a seppuku line. Then he falls onto his back in the cold grass and lays still.

Levi closes the distance too late and locks eyes with the scarecrow as it yanks its blade free from Clyde's body. His finger squeezes the trigger. The beige scarecrow convulses from the impact of bullets as life sprays from the body. Levi turns a full circle to check the area and then kneels beside his fallen comrades. While he closes their vacant stares, he hears more panicked bursts of gunfire and primal screams permeate the battlefield.

On the north side of the tracks, Zulu Everglades walks through the eerie silence and slings his gun over a shoulder until it hangs diagonally from its strap across his back. He reaches into the cargo pockets on each pants leg and withdraws a pair of titanium retractable batons the size of a roll of half dollars. He mashes a button on each handle and flicks his arms out to the side. The batons unfurl and lock into place. Then he ducks and listens to the sounds of the windswept prairie.

Moments later he locks onto movement nearby. Zulu crouches and pokes the batons forward like jousting sticks as he heads towards the sounds. The balled ends of the batons connect six feet away and stand a scythe bladed scarecrow up from its hiding place. The scarecrow swings a bladed hand at Zulu who steps back and smashes his right arm's baton on the scarecrow's wrist. The sound of breaking bone precedes a grunt of anguish from his enemy. Zulu pivots and strikes with his left arm as he arcs a baton into the scarecrows neck and hears the sound of a collarbone snapping.

A second scarecrow emerges with a reaper blade and swings the long stick. Zulu peddles back, slips in the wet mud, lands on his back. He quickly rolls off a shoulder and stabs a knee into the earth as the scarecrow readies another harvest swing. Zulu joins his fists together and swings the melded batons like a sledgehammer. The titanium snaps the reaper blade and the scarecrow turns to flee. Zulu chases him down, splits his hands and brings the rods down on the scarecrow's shoulders. The prey goes rigid with the strike and stumbles through the field spasming like a zombie. The Everglades warrior rejoins his fists and swings a hatchet chop down onto the scarecrow's skull. Then Zulu rises from the motion, flicks blood off the batons and turns to carve a new path.

Outlander and Mallory dash through an open ground prairie graveyard filled with commandos and scarecrows that collided in hand to hand combat after both sides spent their ammo. Mallory catches a wounded scarecrow staggering away and spins it around. The scarecrow stabs at her with a machete and she easily deflects. Outlander catches the wrist holding the machete and holds tight as his other hand shoots out and grabs the scarecrow's throat. He squeezes until the eyes bulge and the rain swept face turns purple. His fingers tighten their grip until he feels the larynx snap in his grasp. Then he lifts his enemy's body and slams it into the mud. He strips the blades from the scarecrow and grasps their wooden handles as he takes the weapons for his own and follows Mallory deeper into the prairie.

Thorpe Cuyahoga and Naomi Shenandoah crouch low on the train's roof, firing constant streams of ammo down into the grassland. An undetected scarecrow rises out of the grass at the front of the train and aims a rifle. A tracer bullet flashes past and slashes a whisker burn across Naomi's remaining pristine cheek. She drops flat on the roof and places a hand to the sting.

Thorpe turns towards the danger and aims but before he can reach the threat, bullets punch into his vest and forearms, standing him up with their force as his gun drops and bounces off the roof. Completely exposed, a bullet hits him in the face and exits out the back of his skull. His body sways for a moment. Then Thorpe collapses and slides off the train to the gravel ground below.

Rain pellets and bullets smack around Naomi as she hugs the roof, avoiding the scarecrow's line of sight. She makes a desperate decision and rolls off the other side of the train, landing between the reeds and the tracks. She quickly aims her gun through the undercarriage of the passenger car as Thorpe's killer rushes her.

Naomi returns fire while rounds ricochet around her. She holds her position and aims until she sees a line of her bullets shatter the scarecrow's legs. The scarecrow bends to the ground and his weapon tumbles under the train. Naomi scoots down the track a little as the man tries to crawl to his rifle. She puts a four shot burst into him and watches his eyes hollow as he sinks into the soil beside Thorpe's body.

On the southern flank, black Dakotaland earth clings to Levi's brown boots as he navigates back to the train through the icy rain falling from the sky. Each droplet like a shard of glass nicking his face. Moisture seeps through crevices of his uniform and coldness bores into him. The hemoglobin in his veins slows and he begins to shiver. Then a shape shifts from the left. He swivels and fires a reckless arc of gunshots. A tan scarecrow convulses as Levi regains control and concentrates the firing. The crude scythe and sickle in its hands go limp and drop to the ground. Then a woman with an Everglades patch across her grey vest passes by. She puts a finger to her mouth for silence and moves past him, further into the tall, swaying grass, stalking the enemy.

A few minutes later, Levi reaches the train and scans along its empty roof. Naomi is gone. He ducks and peers along the undercarriage. Then he spots Thorpe's damaged face laying near a bloody scarecrow. Levi is frozen in place by the ghastly image of another dead friend and watches the rain melt away the paint camouflaged on the scarecrow's face.

The day darkens as storm clouds churn and tint the sky pale green. In the distance, arms of lightning reach down from the sky and jolt the prairie. The idea of warmth seems like an elusive dream. His face hardens into cold stone while his legs grow numb from the burn of crouched movement. He glances up and down the empty tracks in cadence and then decides to cross the line and head north through the tallgrass.

Levi holds his breath as a cloud of noxious smoke drifts by from the lead train's wreckage. Soon he comes upon a death scene of mauled Secret Eden commandos and gunned down scarecrow assassins. After replenishing spent ammo magazines from the pouches of fallen, he resumes looking for survivors within the silent battlefield.

Nearby, Naomi bursts through the wet grass and into open space on the soggy ground. Two Hot Springs soldiers lay with slash marks across their arms and faces next to bullet riddled scarecrows. Naomi turns a full circle and listens for something to orient her to what is still alive and moving. Then a tall scarecrow steps into the field, stops and turns to her. She recognizes the movement of the powerful frame as it strides forward, a wispy white scar across the mohawked scarecrow's forehead that resembles a strand of hair. Coffin Man's skeletal face paint is gone, replaced with streaks of tan camouflage under his dark eyes.

Naomi brushes wet bangs from her eyes and aims her M4 with satisfaction. She presses the trigger. The clicks of an empty ammo magazine clap from the chamber like the start of a funeral dirge hymn. Coffin Man grips a machete as he rushes towards the woman whose cheek he marked a few days ago back in Shenandoah.

She tosses her gun aside and yanks at her grey vest, trying to dislodge her pistol from a load bearing unit's grip. Coffin Man closes in and hurls the machete. Naomi freezes as the sharpened metal tumbles through the air. She closes her eyes expecting death.

The blade pierces the bulletproof vest and knocks her backwards into the wet earth. She lands hard, drops her pistol and slides through the mud while glimpsing the dark sky above with its line of grey tumbling clouds moving like fat worms. Naomi blinks rain water out of her eyes and rolls over, trying to rise as her lungs gulp for breath.

Coffin Man reaches to his waist, unsheathes a scythe, and keeps coming. Naomi sees her pistol laying too far away and makes a decision to stand her ground. She yanks the protruding machete from her vest and rises with it in her palm. Naomi's vision blurs as her jade irises, red from pain and smoke, try to focus on the approaching assassin.

Coffin Man's dark eyes and brown striped camouflage face menacing as he closes in and swings a lethal slash. Naomi dives with the last of her energy. And as she ducks under Coffin Man's curved scythe blade, her right arm shoots out to the side and thrusts the machete forward. She feels a rush of air above her head as she smacks the cold ground, fleeting breath punches out of her lungs and grey unconsciousness pulls her away.

His blade takes a few inches of wet sandy blond hair from the diving target an instant before a flash of silver strikes his leg. Agony stabs through his shin and slices muscle tendons. He howls and crumples to the mud. Coffin Man wills his hand to drop away from the punctured bone and reaches into a pouch slung across his chest. He withdraws a rusty railroad spike souvenir from the day's mayhem and grips the oversized nail. Then he stands and starts shuffling towards Naomi to finish carving her.

Levi Wolff pushes through wild rye and emerges into an open space of matted grass. He instantly recognizes Coffin Man and his massive frame limping towards Naomi as she lies still in the mud. Levi yells with pent up rage as he aims and releases an opening volley.

Coffin Man's elbow shatters and the railroad spike falls into the mud. The Erebus militia commander roars in horror. Levi delivers more rounds, moving the gun barrel's nose slightly with each shot to disperse the damage. Coffin Man jerks violently as metal slugs rip into him, his mohawk bobbing, as the force knocks him onto his back where he writhes and clutches at the open air before going still. Rye stalks above the corpse stain red with thick blood droplets that roll off the stems.

Levi reloads, anchors a knee into the black mud and swivels in search of any sign of approaching danger. A few seconds later, he shoulders his weapon, removes the pistol from his vest and crosses the open ground. Levi picks up the rusty railroad spike and hefts it in his gloved palm, then he drops the talisman into the bloody mud.

Levi steadies himself against a wave of dizziness as the adrenalin fueling him disperses into worry. He takes reluctant steps and kneels in the mud beside Naomi, melting as he hears struggling breaths wheeze out of her throat. Levi rolls his girlfriend over and examines a deep slash in her bulletproof vest. His fingers check for blood through the puncture and find a slight trickle. Naomi's left cheek swells with the fresh mark of brown seared skin. On the other swollen cheek the knife wound's scab is split and bleeding like war paint. He removes his gloves and begins brushing mud from Naomi's face.

Naomi regains consciousness. Her intense green eyes look up at him, "Where's Coffin Man?"

He gently turns her face to the corpse. "Setting off the metal detector at the Gates of Hell."

"Good," she says before slipping back into unconsciousness.

Levi tucks his pistol into its grip on his armored vest, scoops

Naomi up into his arms and leaves the open field. Cold rain patters down onto them and rinses charcoal veins of Dakota earth from Naomi's face as Levi carries her back to the train. Levi leaves the dense prairie grass at his back as he steps onto the hard gravel of the railroad tracks. Haggard Secret Eden operatives are dispersed along the passenger and cargo cars with high ground defensive perches as more survivors emerge from both sides of the prairie.

Outlander spots him and runs over. "How is she?"

"I can't tell how bad her wounds are."

"I'm a medic," Youngblood Springs says as he pushes them aside. "Let me take a look. Outlander, go grab a stretcher."

"What happened?" Youngblood asks as he looks over her wound.

"She caught a bullet or blade in her flak jacket," Levi explains. "It stopped most of the force but not all of it."

"She got grazed on one cheek and has busted stitches on the other one." Youngblood says upon initial inspection. "It's the sternum that I'm worried about. Her breathing is shallow. We need to get her to a medical facility as soon as possible." Youngblood reaches into his pack and withdraws a clear plastic breathing mask with an affixed oxygen canister that he slips over her face. "This will make her more comfortable for the journey." Then he opens a blowout kit, pours sulfa powder into the wound to stave off infection and tapes a thick bandage into place.

"Shenandoah, good to see you alive, but we've gotta go soon," Zulu Everglades calls out as he runs by. "Are there any more survivors out there?"

"I don't know," Levi replies.

Zulu nods, recognizing the combat glazed look in the operative's eyes, and continues on.

Bart hops down from the train and gathers the remaining operatives. "Start off loading cargo. We only need about half the vehicles that we're carrying. Inspect 'em for damage. Keep the best. Destroy the rest."

Levi looks up and down the tracks at the mortality that has taken ahold of Secret Eden's eastern sector. It is as if a river of potential has slowed to a trickle. Five parks now carrying just enough members between them to form two platoons.

Mallory rounds the back of the train with blood on her boots and a mural of splatter across her grey vest.

Levi motions her over. "Naomi is hurt." He rubs the beard stubble across his cheeks as worry lines form on his forehead. "Can you please stay with her while I offload my truck?"

"Of course." Mallory clasps his shoulder. "I won't let her out of my sight."

Outlander returns with a stretcher. "Where is Clyde? Anybody seen him?"

"He was cut up real bad," Levi says and watches the sheriff grind his teeth and spit a wad of tobacco onto the blood speckled ground. "He didn't make it."

Outlander nods gravely. "I'm gonna go check the lead train for survivors."

Levi spots a stitch of bullet holes across the doors of his truck and patches them with duct tape before lowering the bulkheads, pulling the slat rails and driving off the flatcar. Then he reaches into a bag of dried stores and chews on a licorice stick to calm his nerves.

The severely diminished caravan of a dozen vehicles trench their way through the soaked fields of South Dakota as lightning stabs the ground. They head towards a highway in the distance where the plateau erodes into serrated Badlands buttes layered with black pierre shale from an ancient seabed, yellow ocher, grey chadron and tan brule sediment from when the forests gave way to savannah, and topped by a layer of volcanic rockyford ash.

A few miles down the road a faded brown sign with chipped

white lettering welcomes the eastern survivors to Badlands National Park. Thirty vehicles and a pack of a hundred personnel from the Voyaguer, Isle Royale and Badlands tribes wait at the entrance. A battle worn Levi watches Youngblood accompany Zulu and Outlander to the park's entrance. Youngblood does not linger for long.

"What about the medical facility?" Levi asks when Youngblood returns.

"They don't have anything that's not in this vehicle as well. The treatment Naomi needs is further up the road."

"How far?" Levi asks.

"It's close by, but the weather's getting worse."

Levi peers out at an endless shadow spreading across the expanse of sky. He slams his fists against the steering wheel in despair.

"Just follow Outlander and Mallory's truck and pray for her," Youngblood says. "Naomi is resting in the back. I'm taking care of her. Gave her a morphine stick. She's wounded but she's gonna live, man."

The convoy pulls out of the park entrance and merges west on I-90, following the straight road into the rumbling thunder of the storm for miles before exiting off Route 36 near the frontier town of Deadwood and driving inside a mountain tunnel to shelter. The survivors hunker down and take the opportunity to rest as destructive winds and tornado funnels spin across the landscape. With vehicles blocking each entrance and a storm bearing down outside, they gather around a bonfire in the center of the tunnel and trade regional stories from the past few weeks while they clean their weapons and gear.

Naomi's stretcher sits near a kerosene lantern, with Levi beside her, holding her hand and waiting for color to flood back into her pale face. Youngblood naps nearby so that he can take the late shift.

Mallory comes over and sits beside Levi. "It wasn't supposed to be like this, but we have to keep moving."

"What's up the road, Mallory?"

"An outpost containing a hidden tribe."

"Will they watch after her?"

"Yes," she says as he looks down at Naomi.

"Why all the mystery?"

"The sacred Black Hills of South Dakota are becoming the epicenter of American Indian culture. The Embassy of Tribal Nations has moved their flags and operations out here from D.C.," she says as she reaches over to the lantern and dims the light. "The elders of all of the gathered tribes are compiling a unified collection of Native beliefs into a tribal record. Outlander and the other sheriffs didn't want to endanger them by announcing a sovereign and independent Secret Eden tribe."

Levi stays silent, too exhausted to fully process the information.

"I spent part of my childhood in Barrow, Alaska," Mallory says. "My father told me a story once about a lost Inupiat hunter who was adrift for days in the Arctic Ocean. The currents would carry his canoe close to shore, but not close enough to swim for it in the cold waters. So he kept watch and waited for his fate to either push him towards land or farther out to sea." She reaches down and plucks a couple of tiny rocks from the pavement, bouncing them slightly in her palm. "And every so often, the hunter would reach down to the still water of a slack tide and lightly touch the flattened palm of his hand to the ocean surface, only pulling it back when he felt the slightest feeling of moisture along the tip of his skin. Then he would lift his hand and cup the drops with his fingers pointing down like a claw." She mimics the words as the pebbles tumble as if falling through a chute. "The wise hunter was able to stave off dehydration and ultimately survive by letting drops of freshwater molecules which form along the top layer of the Arctic Ocean's surface trickle down his thirsty throat one carefully timed motion at a time. Avoiding saltwater." Mallory rises to her feet. "Humans are resilient creatures. Remember that when you look at her and the road ahead." And then she fades into the tunnel's shadows.

Levi sits by the lantern's faint flame in silence for a long time. His eyelids heavy with fatigue. Then just as he begins to nod off, he feels Naomi squeeze his hand and intertwine her fingers with his.

THE BLACK HILLS

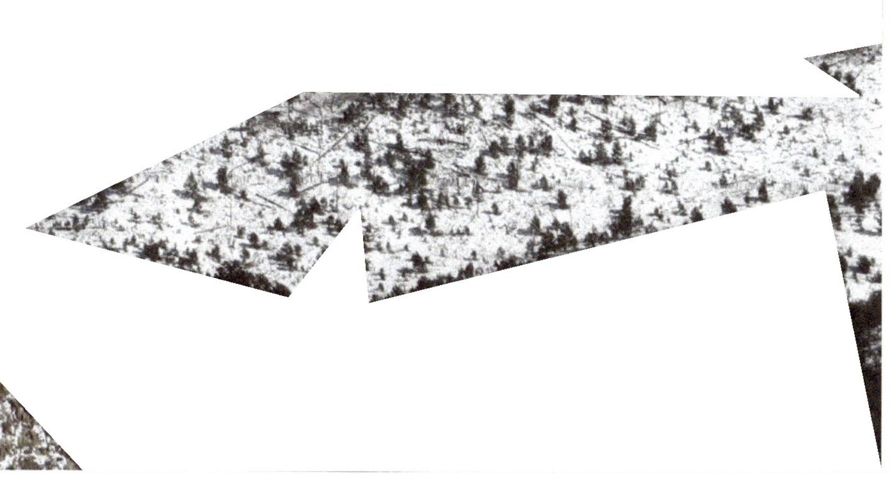

Day 24

Riders sit atop powerful horses at the entrance, war paint etched across their faces, and long hair the color of raven feathers catching in the wind. Behind them, a mile off in the distance, the sculpted granite arm of the world's tallest monument points to the sacred area to remind the spirit of a people that their lands are where their dead lay buried.

A tall man from the hidden tribe dismounts and walks forward. Outlander climbs out of the jeep to meet him. They reach each other and clasp shoulders.

"*Mitakuye Oyasin,*" Outlander says in Dakota language.

"*Mitakuye Oyasin,*" Aakicita Sioux replies as he peers along the line of transport vehicles, searching for more men and women. "How far back is the rest of your force?"

"We're all that's left. It's been a hard road." Outlander shakes his head with sorrow. "We were attacked at Shenandoah and again in the Badlands. Both times were a bloodbath."

"Do you have wounded that require medical treatment?" Aakicita asks.

"Yes, a few. We patched them up last night as best we could. But some will not be able to travel on."

"Follow us to the community health center." The American Indian points down the road. "Have your men and women pass through the facility first to get checked out. Anyone that needs to stay, may stay as long as it takes for them to heal."

"Thank you," Outlander says as he stares at the forest of ponderosa pine and juniper trees on the surrounding hills.

"There is a snowstorm blowing in. We should leave before it takes hold. And grab hot showers. Once everyone is tended to, gather the sheriffs." Aakicita points up to the mountain. "The elders are up there in a longhouse built across the monument's arm. They want to talk with us. They speak of *tokata*, the future, being uncertain. There has been much discussion on whether or not the night rainbows will spark a return to the natural way. There are also strange things happening in the surrounding area. Patrols have gone missing. The lines leading into Yellowstone Valley have been breached. An enemy is traveling with government uniforms. Everything is speeding up, old friend."

Outlander nods agreement and returns to his truck as Aakicita mounts his horse and grabs the reigns. The riders gallop down a long straight path with the eastern band of Secret Eden following.

A half hour later, Levi keeps a close eye on Naomi while a medicine woman finishes examining her and applies a torch flower salve to the wound.

"She is going to be okay," the doctor says. "It will just take time for her cartilage to heal. Why don't you go grab a hot shower?"

"Thank you, ma'am." Levi starts to go but turns back. "This means more to me than I can adequately convey." The woman smiles and pats his hand until his worried eyes relax.

Day becomes night while the Secret Eden and American Indian tribes share stories around scattered campfires. The sheriffs split off. Aakicita Sioux, Zulu Everglades, Marston Voyaguer, Windigo Royale, Izzy Badlands and Outlander Shenandoah hike up the mountain through falling snow beneath a hazy moon.

When they crest the mountain and reach the long carved arm of the monument, they are led into a tent flowing with warmth from heated rocks in a fire pit. The structure layered with animal pelts to provide a seal against the wind. Inside, elders gathered from across the country, sit on pegmatite granite rock stumps blasted from the mountain. The sheriffs stand as the elders beat deerskin drums and chant a rhythm to the heart of the gathering. Aakicita calls out the names of each visitor and an elder inscribes them on a birch bark scroll painted with the words *wichasta ohuze*, warrior mystics.

Down below the mountain, Levi watches Naomi rest. Her puffy lips pressing air in an out in soft wisps. She wakes when he kisses her on the forehead and takes a long look at the rucksack and slung gun on his shoulders before meeting his eyes. "I'm not ready to say goodbye to you yet," she whispers.

"The trucks are being restocked. It'll be time to move on soon." Then Levi pauses and cocks his head to the side, distracted by something new. "Did you get a haircut?"

"A scythe took a few inches from one side in the Badlands," she says with a coy smile, "so I asked the nurse to even it up." Moments pass and Naomi reaches up to touch Levi's wounded cheek. "Just make sure you survive so that we can find each other again." She begins to gently paint his face with her fingertips. He starts to speak but she puts her hand to his mouth. "You're so close to the end. Don't die out there. See it through and then we'll find our bliss."

"You and me," he says as he leans down to give her a kiss goodbye. "Our canvas is not complete."

Mallory enters the room. "I'm sorry Levi, but it's time to go. The sheriffs are coming down the mountain. We need you outside. Naomi, rest and heal up so that you can rejoin us down the road. Until then, take care."

"Thanks. You, too."

Levi reluctantly pulls away from Naomi, struggling to suppress the desire to stay with her until she is whole again. He turns in the doorway to absorb the affection in her eyes as her lashes blink away a tear.

"Dream about me," she says. "Maybe I'll meet you there some night."

"I'll see you soon." And then he walks away. Outside, he heads to the caravan as ten Black Hills vehicles pull up. Levi climbs in his truck and spots a hitchhiking Everglades sheriff sitting in the shotgun seat beside him, chewing on a prairie grass stem.

At dawn, a weather beaten sign welcomes the convoy to Wyoming as they cross the state line and maneuver along slow snowy roads winding through the Rockies. Gillette pastureland and open coal pits pass by as they cut through the vast ranches of Sheridan County. They rest for a few hours in an empty rodeo ring in the town of Cody. Then drive parallel to the flowing Shoshone River with sagebrush at its banks and hoodoos perched above the canyon walls of the Sylvan Pass, moving through scenic wonders in giant counties. Yellowstone's east entrance forty miles away and the fulcrum of the journey upon them.

YELLOWSTONE

Day 26

On the eastern boundary, park rangers move down the long row of vehicles, inspecting vest patches and checking names on clipboards.

"Hurry up," Outlander calls. "Then seal the gate and let nothing through."

The convoy passes through the gates and into an epic wilderness where a hypnotic road carves the snow across panoramic vistas. Their line rips an asphalt seam through an endless white fold, passing by frozen waterfalls of cold beauty and sheets of ice floating down the Yellowstone River. Glazed conifer forests of engelmann spruce, subalpine fir and lodgepole pine spear the Rocky Mountains for miles into the distance. The desolate billowy fields appear absent of wildlife due to hibernation and migration, until an elk herd shatters the quiet landscape with bugling songs that resemble the call of whales through vast ocean waters.

An abandoned tourist settlement along Lake Yellowstone marks the road with a reminder of their mission. Eight men and women wearing dull black helmets and pea coats perch on snow mobiles with menacing weapons in their grip beside a pallet of riot shields. Hydrothermal steam blows up from the banks of the lake, moves across the road, and through a section of wildfire scorched forest, blotting out the view in a sulfur haze. The eastern tribes ready their weapons as the line crawls to a stop. A man walks through the heated cloud, removes his helmet, and approaches Outlander's truck.

Outlander gets out and motions for Zulu and Izzy to join him on the road. They trudge through the snow and meet up with sheriff Echo Dune who they last saw at White Sands, while the rest of the line watches the woods for signs of ambush.

"Outlander, where's the rest of the eastern force?" the nomadic pack's emissary asks.

"We're what's left of it," he says. "We were attacked twice on the way here. We've suffered heavy casualties. Down to a third of our intended size."

Echo's face tightens as snowflakes dust his red beard. "I was ordered here by Fairchild Arch to intercept you and warn you about our situation before you move on. It's grim. The southern region was gutted at our rendezvous down the road in Jackson Hole. Three entire tribes are gone. The others depleted."

"How?" Outlander demands.

"By a militia of mercenaries who swelled their ranks with cannon fodder. They call themselves the Akkad." Echo looks past them along the winding road leading in from the east. "Were you followed?"

"No, the tail is clear. We killed our trackers in the Badlands," Outlander says.

"Look, we don't have much time. Something's wrong. Yellowstone is about to be under siege." Echo Dune looks back along the road leading west with uncertainty. "The Teton tribe is clearing our path in. We're going to lead you back along our trail. Be ready. The Battle of Yellowstone is about to begin." Then he turns and jogs back to his snow mobile.

Outlander gathers the other sheriffs and orders them to spread Echo's warning through the entire line as they pass out the riot shields. Then he climbs back into his truck and follows Echo towards the core of Secret Eden.

The village of West Thumb is in ruin on the edge of Lake Yellowstone. Invaders and defenders scatter the ground amid burned out buildings and vehicles. The eastern convoy rolls by cautiously and climbs the plateau to the Upper Basin. They traverse the Continental Divide and head towards park's command node atop the largest caldera on Earth. The terrain changes to steaming geysers and bubbling pools of mud while a storm in the atmosphere sends flickers of lightning across the sky.

A battered sign for Old Faithful Inn flashes by as the eastern tribes crest a hill and dip onto a long winding road leading down into the basin. One mile to go. The column decelerates and fans out in a wide line across the slope to survey an open field. Calamity is upon the area. Thick lines of blacktop cut an iris through the snow where intersecting tribes and an enemy force converged in a smash mouth demolition of pulsion proof machines. A shallow graveyard of bodies spreads through charred wreckage of crumpled metal squirts industrial bloods of fluid and fuel on the precious land. And beyond the carnage, a ring of fire burns through a wagon train of vehicles encircling the lodge, sending acrid black smoke billowing up into the sky in dark plumes that battle the pristine geysers for supremacy.

The center of the basin's eye contains a towering lodge. Below its slanted roofs, gunners from both sides are locked in a duel with heavy machine guns as a wave of two hundred camouflage attackers pour through breaches in the defensive perimeter of the Old Faithful Inn and descend on the tattered platoons of

Secret Eden. The threat of being overrun gathers on the doorstep. Ruthless violence rages. Gun muzzles swivel and sweep chaos as searing bullets scoop wooden chunks out of the structure and drop men and women as metal slugs bore into flesh.

Up on the slope, snow mobiles and all terrain trucks mash pedals and feed fuel to engines. Snow chained tires dig into winter ground like claws. Two hundred Secret Eden sheriffs and operatives build speed down the hill and surge across the open field of dry snow to close within a half mile of the inn.

Bullets begin to career in and slap the charging vehicles, cobwebbing the windshields. A quarter mile to go. The convoy spreads out in combat intervals to create lanes of space. One hundred yards. The shifting battlefield approaches. Fifty yards. The eastern sector stampedes into the Battle of Yellowstone.

Levi brakes and bucks against the seatbelt as his truck slides to a stop in the snow. Powder kicks up over the grill and spreads across the windshield as he releases his belt and flings his door open. He hops out and hits the ground with his weapon in one hand and riot shield in the other.

The Badlands, Royale and Voyaguer drivers shove fuel canisters down into the floorboards of their vehicles to mash the gas pedals into acceleration. Their troops roll out the doors into soft snow to join their brethren as staggered metal battering rams ghost ride across the terrain like zebra stripes.

Secret Eden's eastern region enters the grinder of combat on foot with guns blazing as the Akkad attackers return fire that chips away at their line. Up ahead, revved ghost riding vehicles bulldoze Akkad snow mobiles armed with pillion scat snipers. Smashed vehicles flip upside down, hoofs up with tires and tracks spinning in the air. Shards tear through the air from the collisions and detonations.

Shrapnel embeds in Levi's riot shield as he runs and blends in with the tribes moving across the killing field. He reaches the edge of the ring of fire where burning figures doused in exploded fuel flail around before they drop to the snow and lay still. Levi shovels steady breaths into his lungs as he swivels his gun, releasing wild staccato bursts of gunfire at the diminishing enemy force. The wind kicks up snow and blurs visibility. He loses sight of Mallory, Outlander, and Bart as the whistle of hot lead whizzes by, riding the cold wind.

The remaining Akkad soldiers abandon their defense against the arriving eastern tribes, turn and breach the ground floor of the lodge. The hallways of the inn light up as automatic gunfire rips the air to form a grisly halo.

The eastern tribes raise their shields, reload their weapons, and march towards wooden steps leading up to the Old Faithful Inn. The Akkad turn from their assault on the lodge and collide with the eastern platoons. Firefights rip through the opposing forces with a frenzy of orange tracers lancing through the air. Punctured bodies drop through a haze of cordite as ammunition magazines empty. Hand to hand combat follows.

Zulu releases his telescoping batons and starts cracking masks and shattering bones. Levi passes by a comrade who is clutching a ghastly wound on her neck with blood stained gloves. He reaches to grab her, but she drops to the ground and lays pale and still.

Bart runs for the steps and is suddenly smacked backwards by a sledgehammer of shotgun fire from a busted window. He lands and skids to a halt with smoking shards of metal sticking out of his shredded flak jacket. Bart rolls over onto his side and coughs thick blood past the whiskers of his handlebar mustache as he tries to crawls forward. Then he slows as his eyes lock into a lifeless stare and his head dips into the snow.

Levi becomes unhinged as he watches his friend fall. He smacks in a fresh mag of ammo and unleashes a full clip of bullets in an arc of rapid fire at the row of windows above. When his gun clicks empty Mallory grabs him and drags him stubbornly to cover below the inn's porch steps. She pulls him close. "Hold it together," she shouts as flecks of snow land around her fierce eyes. Then she lets go and rushes up the steps.

As Levi tries to reload, a wounded mind hunter falls from the deck above and begins to rise. Youngblood appears beside him, extends his gun and puts double shots into the man's skull before running up the steps after Mallory. Levi moves to follow but two bullets fired from the breached lodge strike his bulletproof vest. The force of the dual impact punches him onto his back. For a long moment he clutches his chest with the haunting feeling that his lungs have been crushed. Despite the agony, he rolls over in the snow and rises as a third bullet grazes his left forearm. He stumbles to cover against the side of the porch steps and rips the stitches in his cheek rip open as he breathes hard breaths back into his chest. Danger and confusion close in. The battle's shifting trajectories too fast to process.

Then Outlander and Zulu appear above him and provide defensive fire into the haze as they lift him up. Levi grimaces as adrenalin pumps the pain away from the smoking bullet holes in his vest.

Gunfire claps through air all around them as Outlander reloads. Then he sets his gun down, grabs Levi's weapon, ejects the empty mag, slaps in a fresh one, and taps the bottom of the cold cartridge to lock it in place. "You ready?" he asks as he tosses the weapon back.

Levi digs his boots into the icy ground and nods. Outlander peers around the edge of the porch and spots Zulu and Echo rushing the steps. Levi follows Outlander out of the cover and squeezes off bursts of fire. Then they take the steps side by side and reach the porch of Old Faithful Inn.

A gutshot mind hunter pushes out from under a pile of bodies and raises a machine gun. Outlander turns to the rising threat just as a spear of automatic gunfire hits his shield. The bonded plastic buckles against the bullets and bends away in their force. His ribs receive one shot at close range as the mercenary's gun clicks empty. Outlander slumps to his knees and falls sideways onto the porch.

Time sinks into slow motion as Levi rushes the attacker and puts point blank bullets into the mind hunter. Then Levi turns and slides through a small pool of maroon blood spreading across the wooden planks and grabs Outlander. The sheriff of Shenandoah tries to blink stability back into his torn body as the fierce quickness of battle bends and falters around them. Black Hills commandos rush by and secure the area while Outlander's eyes become faint and a moment later his paling face becomes slack as he passes out, his fate in the balance.

"I need to get him to surgery quickly." Aakicita hefts Outlander up over his shoulder and aims his machine gun forward. "There is a medical clinic in the old gift store. Tell Mallory."

Levi follows them into the lodge and meets Zulu in the scarred hallway, bodies from both sides at their feet.

"Keep moving," the Cajun yells as they move cautiously into the inn's cavernous lobby. "Let's get to the rally point."

Cold survivors from the gathered in tribes stare around a den where giant log columns reach up into the rafters and brace a network of wooden walkways and staircases that connect five floors of rooms. They stand in trance like exhaustion, catching their breath and trying to slow the pounding beat of their hearts in the aftermath of the violence.

The Yellowstone platoon descends from their gunner positions on the upper floors, carrying fire extinguishers along with their guns as they clomp along the planks. Down below, triage care takes form. Secret Eden's lightly wounded are brought close to the fireplace as medics tend to them and apply tourniquets. Fallen brothers and sisters are laid reverently along the carpet in an adjoining room off the lobby that transforms into a makeshift morgue.

When the Yellowstone operatives arrive on the ground floor they begin dragging the dead invaders out of the room and toss the bodies over the porch railing into a heap below. Afterwards, they walk the basin performing a dead check. Occasional gunshots pop as they execute the last of the mercenaries entombed in the snow.

A tall woman with long straight black hair looks around the room at the survivors. "My name is Absaroka. I'm the sheriff of Yellowstone," she shouts with a voice heavy with authority. "Once we secure the perimeter, start sending the sheriffs and operatives down one by one for debriefing." Then she turns her gaze upon three prisoners being held in the center of the room on a bloody carpet. Absaroka moves to the fireplace and digs two wrought iron implements into glowing coals. "Bring them closer," she says over her shoulder.

Her soldiers haul a badly wounded man forward. But before he can face Absaroka he convulses and collapses to the floor. A soldier places two fingers to the man's neck and looks up as he shakes his head. Absaroka studies the dead man's face a moment and shrugs. "Toss him outside," she says with a flick of her head. Then she turns to the second captive. A short muscular man with shaggy hair and a thick beard. "What is your rank?"

"I'm just a foot soldier," Joe Rusk stammers, feigning fear. "A month ago I was a drifter with nowhere else to go, just trying to survive the winter."

Absaroka shakes her head. "Then you can't help me." She removes a red hot crowbar from the fire and impales the man. The remaining captive pulls his chin from his chest and looks into her eyes as soldiers drag the body outside and drop it off the porch.

"What's your name?"

"Barrick Akkad," he says with eerie calm. "And the man you just killed was far more than a foot soldier."

"Search him."

When the Yellowstone men rip Akkad's bulletproof vest from his chest a piece of flat wood falls onto the floor. Absaroka leans down and examines the carved card of a cyclops skeleton holding a celestial globe of warring constellations. "What is this?" her voice a whip.

"A sign of things to come," Akkad says. "Defcon Denver will be infiltrated."

Absaroka moves back to the fireplace and removes a log grabber from the heated belly of the chimney. The glowing curved ends of the black iron snap open like molten jaws. "When these get hot enough, they will bore right through to the bone. The steel rod cauterizes the wound but amplifies the pain. That'll give us extra time together."

"Lady, you don't know the places I've been and the things I've done to survive." Akkad shows no emotion. His pale blond hair and translucent eyebrows framing piercing dark brown eyes. "If you're gonna torture me, then get to it."

"Okay then." Absaroka nods to four of her platoon. "Pin 'em down."

They restrain Akkad's thrashing attempts to break free. Absaroka takes her knife out, cuts the laces of the man's combat boot, and removes the shoe. Then picks up the searing pincers that are engraving the lodge floor and thrusts them onto his heel, locking each half moon scissor in place. Akkad hollers as singed hair and burning flesh smoke up from his ankle.

Then Absaroka releases the iron pincers and flings them towards the fireplace. "Who are you?" She waits for his agony to subside into a lucid throb.

"The American establishment is at war with itself." Barrick Akkad cusses the flashing pain ringing the leg. "You're on one side. And I'm on the other," he says through clenched teeth. "When this is all over, whoever wins becomes the good guys, and whoever loses becomes the bad guys. It's a fight for the future."

Absaroka motions for him to continue. "What is this wooden card?"

"Eighty eight interlocking tarot cards were cut from a mahogany tree in the tropical jungle of Papua New Guinea near the Cyclops Mountains. Then the cards were gifted." His eyes not wavering from Absaroka's stare. "It was given to me by a great man. A man who died. But not before setting a plan in motion."

"Who else do you know that has one of these cards?" Absaroka asks.

Barrick Akkad shakes his head, puffs a breath of pain and inhales slowly. "The other warlords will reveal themselves in due time."

"You'll be bone and gristle by this time tomorrow." Absaroka turns to the Yellowstone platoon. "Take him outside. I want a full interrogation performed." Her voice drips revenge as she relays the orders. "Then tie him to a tree and leave him to be torn to pieces by wild animals." Then she walks to a door on the far side of the room and the sheriffs follow her down into the basement.

A Yellowstone medic moves down the line and crouches in front of Levi.

"Where are you injured, Shenandoah?"

He shows her his wounds and she sets to work on them. She removes the bloody bandage from his cheek and sprays stinging antiseptic into the busted stitches of the knife cut. Then staples fresh stitches into his skin before slapping a clean bandage on.

Echo Dune comes over after the medic moves down the line. He sits down beside Levi and does not say anything as he runs his hands through his red beard to smooth out the manic strands of hair.

Levi looks over at him. "How many of your riders made it through?"

Echo stares straight ahead. "Just me."

Levi closes his eyes and rests while he waits for his debriefing.

Nearby Mallory exits the medic station after watching Outlander undergo surgery to remove the bullet. Her smooth pale cheeks stream moisture as she walks out onto the back porch facing Old Faithful geyser. She sits on a bench as snowflakes hover like crystal fireflies and stares across the basin while the roughly one hundred and twenty surviving members of Secret Eden set up a new perimeter. Mallory stays there in silence and listens to the wind of memory as she prays for Outlander to survive.

An hour later, the air in the cellar is cold and dry. Wine bottles and files cram racks throughout the room. A fire wanes in its hearth atop a mound of burned paper. On a ledge above the fireplace, a pendulum clock's fried mechanical hands point straight up in doomsday pose. The sheriff of Yellowstone motions for Levi to sit with her at an old wooden table that holds a block of cheese, half a loaf of bread, a wine bottle and a goblet.

"Name, please."

"Levi Wolff from Shenandoah."

"Do you know why Secret Eden had to travel to Yellowstone?"

"No, I don't. But I watched a lot of good people die trying to get here."

"Go on and grab a bite to eat." She pours him a glass of wine. "You must be hungry."

"I'm not." Levi's eyes stay on her, waiting for a reason. "Do you have whiskey?"

Absaroka nods to a shelf over Levi's shoulder. "Help yourself."

He grabs a bottle and a short bourbon glass, pops the cork and pours a tall drink to warm himself up.

"The tribes were gathered here because..." Her throat tightens as she gathers her fatigue back into a tight mask that creases the features of her beautiful face with its lines of Crow Indian heritage. "Soon we will disperse. Most of the survivors will head to the Broadmoor complex beside NORAD in Colorado Springs to help lead the recovery as emissaries. Many of the sheriffs will command roaming recon expeditions to No Man's Land. Places like the Vegas ghost town to root out resistance movements of renegades that have holed up in the abandoned casinos. Each of us will be carrying new assignments in this new world. And operatives will travel with us." She walks to a near empty shelf, retrieves an accordion file folder and sets it on the table. "I've got the files here from your tribe. How many of you survived?"

"Just four of us." Levi chokes on the words.

"Too many have been lost," Absaroka sinks back into her chair and reaches into the Shenandoah folder. "I have had to burn scores of files." Her haggard eyes dip to the files in her hands. "What are the other survivors' names?"

"Naomi, Outlander and Mallory." He pauses. "I think Outlander. He's in surgery." Absaroka nods gravely. "Naomi didn't make it this far though. She's healing in the Black Hills from wounds she sustained in the Badlands."

"We need everyone. When she's ready to travel, we'll bring her to Colorado. That is, if she is willing." Absaroka puts the other files in the folder, rises, and tosses them onto the burning logs. "This is to protect their surviving families." Tiny rivers of fire swell and swallow the sheets. Life stories and lost paths ebb in an aqua flame that shrivels until it wafts smokes and lingering sparks vanish. She returns to the table and flips open Levi's file. After a moment, she looks up. "Levi Wolff, it says here that you carry a liberty dollar map."

He nods to confirm the background details.

"It will take years to rebuild what existed before the solar flares and electromagnetic pulse bombs. Perhaps a generation or more." The sheriff of Yellowstone removes an envelope from the back of his file and tears it open. "Before the storm, we were a world leading culture in virtually every field of knowledge." She reads the letter and sets it face down on the table. "Regardless of what happens next, remember that America was once a paranormal nation. We can be that again."

He listens to the words and sadness wells up over all that has happened to his country in such a short time.

"Levi, we still need you." She closes his file. "Would you be willing to stay on with us?"

"I don't know. I'm tired." Levi grows uneasy at the thought and shifts in his chair as anxiety kicks into high gear. "I need some time to think about it." He yearns to release his stress along the national forest trails that envelop his family's secluded homestead, close to where he went to camp as a kid. To run through a warm sunshine beside soothing brooks until he feels right again. To wait for the whippoorwill to sing the arrival of spring. To sit in a forest of tall trees, taking his time to make the decision at an old mill's water wheel. "I've been traveling for too long. I want to go home and see my family and then decide. I can't make that decision here."

"We're only asking for a season." Absaroka picks up the letter. "No more than two. And it can be close to Alabama or even in your home state. Help is needed everywhere."

"Can Naomi come with me?" He tears off a bite of bread and chases it down with a sip of whiskey.

Absaroka reaches for Naomi's file and removes an envelope from it. She breaks the seal and reads the letter for a moment before returning it to its place. "It says here that Naomi has been assigned to a diplomatic mission that will trek up to the borderlands at Glacier. It's a pre designated spot where Secret Eden and the Mounties are supposed to rendezvous to assess each nation's situation. Perhaps you could join Naomi on her mission."

"Look, I'm not ready to head back into what I've just come through. I need time. I want her to come home with me."

Absaroka's eyes convey understanding as she reaches down to her pack and withdraws a black velvet pouch. She opens the string at the mouth and removes two items. She hands Levi a sapphire blue bead and an obsidian black band. Levi studies the strange carvings across the surface of the bead, tracing his fingers along the band's thin ridges and indentions.

"This is your mark of authenticity. It uses an ancient method," she says. "When the bead is dipped in ink and aligned with the band, insert a thin piece of parchment between the two and roll the bead across the surface to produce an image."

"What kind of image?"

"Give it a try," she advises. "You'll see."

Levi fastens the black band across the fading handcuff bruise ringing his wrist. Next, he soaks the blue bead in the wine goblet while he tears a sliver from his coda letter. Then he combines the three objects and scribes the symbol of his journey from Hawaii to Shenandoah to Yellowstone. The grape ink reveals the stars of the Orion constellation in an X-formation.

"Thread the bead through that chain around your neck," she instructs. "They are two parts of a cylinder seal that will validate your identity as a scribe of Secret Eden." Absaroka watches him smile for the first time.

"Thank you," he says when he looks up.

Her eyes sparkle with compassion.

"Why are we leaving Yellowstone? Can't we stay here a while?" he asks. "We've got wounded that need time to recuperate."

"This park rests atop a super volcano. Yellowstone is the site of one of the most destructive eruptions in history." The sheriff clasps her hands on the table. "With all the seismology gear ruined, we no longer have a warning system for this hibernating volcano."

"Then why even gather us here?" Levi asks.

"Because Yellowstone is the closest thing to the Garden of Eden in existence. It was a matter of faith that brought us here, but that doesn't mean we're going to tempt fate by lingering."

"I understand," Levi says as he stands. "Look, if I'm up for another round of this, I'll let you know soon. If I'm not, I will want to fade back into the privacy I grew accustomed to in the parks."

"You're free Levi, you always have been."

"I think I'll take a walk now to clear my mind."

"Levi, thank you." Sheriff Absaroka rises and extends her hand. "I wish we could say and do more, but perhaps we can in time." They shake hands. "You've got some time to decide where you want to go from here." She flicks her head towards the stairs. "Head on up and rest while we finish these debriefings."

Outside, Levi approaches Mallory's bench as dusk hovers in the freezing air and snow falls on the shoulders of her pea coat like tiny feathers.

She looks up and then she glances at the slight tremor in his hands. "When did those start?"

"After my detour to the Forgotten Coast. They come and go. They'll get better once I get some rest." Levi looks out at the sunset painting dark shades into the sky and shoves his hands into his jean pockets to smother the movement.

"Those are combat tremors." Mallory shakes her head. "They'll take time." She drops her eyes to the ground. "I am never going to stop missing him if he fades. I don't know if Will is going to survive past surgery, Levi. It's touch and go. Youngblood is in there helping. Distract me. Tell me about the trip from California to New Orleans. I know Will. He skipped over the dangerous parts."

Levi sits beside Mallory and tells her of the day he arrived in Death Valley, about Arizona, New Mexico, the raid in Texas, and the haunted voyage down the Mississippi River. Stories that carry them to the moment when she reunited with Outlander. Then he pauses until it seems okay to ask a question he has been harboring.

"Sheriff Absaroka was holding something back. I could tell. Why did Secret Eden's tribes have to travel out of their parks to converge here at Yellowstone?"

"Because we are the wild card that was shuffled into this whole equation. Created to deal with the unforeseen. A fallback plan for that which could not be predicted. We are an all-volunteer force that traveled all the way here to Yellowstone. There are no phones. No computers. The only secure way for us to communicate is in person. Like the old Pony Express carrying messages to remote outposts. Now our mission is to go out into the darkness."

Levi digests her words and sits there watching dusk fall on the basin.

"I've been to Yellowstone once before." Mallory points north. "There are two hot springs up the road where vivid sapphire blue pools are surrounded by green, yellow, and orange rings of algae. The Grand Prismatic Spring and Morning Glory are exact replicas of the Ring Nebula in the Lyra constellation in space." She pauses and looks into his eyes. "One night in Alaska, I drove out to Point Barrow to watch the Northern Lights flare. And I began to wonder if the labyrinth of the human mind and map of the universe are related. If each design could be part of a single fathomable map. Like each galaxy's light corresponding to a scaled neuron within our own minds."

"I'd have to think about that another time," Levi deflects. "Been a long year."

Mallory puts her elbows on her knees and places her chin in her hands. "I'm too sad to feel anything but pain right now."

"I'm so tired, I'm numb." He stands and moves away from the bench so that the cold wind can help keep him awake.

Mallory looks over at him. "Mystics say that those who have crossed between worlds are restless because they have existed in two places, but now must exist in one while waiting for the other."

"I don't understand the context," Levi says and resumes pacing.

"Yes, you do." Mallory's expression of certainty stays on him. "I spent my nights in Shenandoah with Outlander. He was especially interested in your file because of a near-death experience that showed up in your background check. He showed me your file, Levi."

Before he can reply, the Old Faithful geyser sputters to life. A jet of water emerges from the earth, erupting like an exhale from a massive whale. They watch the mesmerizing plume of boiling water extend a hundred feet in the air and lift in the wind. Precious time passes in the world's first national park as the iconic geyser spouts and paints the sky with mist. They forget it all for a few minutes until Old Faithful recedes into the ground and the basin grows still again.

"So what now?" he asks.

"We preserve the Constitution and pick up the pieces. But first we have to survive the winter."

"Something still seems to be missing."

"Bad things are coming in the darkness." Mallory pauses to collect her thoughts. "The sheriffs aren't supposed to say anything to the operatives yet but…"

"What is it?" Levi interrupts.

"Are you sure? It's been a rough few days. You still have time to walk away from all this." Mallory glances over at him. "You've done enough. It's okay now to just live out the rest of your days in peace some place where it's safe."

"I'm here and I'm sure," Levi answers. "What's wrong?"

"It has to do with that letter Outlander received from Echo

Dune at White Sands." Mallory turns to face him. "The Aurora Terra solar flares' subatomic particles have somehow altered the weapons grade nuclear material."

Levi takes a step back and rubs the palm of his hand over his eyes, trying to stave off a migraine while absorbing the implications. "What do you mean?"

"I'm not sure what I mean," Mallory shrugs. "All we know is that a cosmic alchemy has occurred. The nuclear arsenal is damaged. Severely damaged. All of the bombs inspected are ruined. None appear to be surviving the storm's transmutation."

"So you're telling me we no longer have a nuclear deterrent?"

"The rules of warfare have changed. They've been dialed back to pre-1945 and beyond. Earth's transuranic elements past 88 on the periodic table have been scrambled somehow. We're vulnerable. If word gets out, armies will march on America to hit us before we can stand back up."

Levi turns away from Mallory and looks into the distance, "And why won't the current bombs work?"

"Critical mass, the amount needed for detonation and chain reaction, can no longer be reached," Mallory explains as she stoops down and places a gloved finger in the snow. "The weapons grade enrichment process vacillates between material consisting of yellowcake from uranium oxide." Her finger draws the letters UO. "And white crystals from uranium fluoride." Her hand moves to the right and draws UF. "The qualities are different now."

Levi's pulse rises. "How different?"

"The altered substance now found in our nuclear bombs is a yellow stone made of uranium fluoride oxide."

Levis forms the chemical letters in his mind as Mallory draws new letters in the snow that flash like a neon sign. UFO. An astonished Levi feels his knees weaken and takes a seat on the bench. They sit in silence for a moment as the wind rustles the evergreen trees and the sun slides behind the horizon, flooding the area in a burnt orange glow.

"I know it's too much to take in. Our world is totally different now in more than one way. No electricity. No nuclear weapons. A new dark age swarming with chaos out there among the wastelands of civilization."

"What is Defcon Denver going to do?" Levi asks.

"That decision will be controlled by the surviving government leaders that reach the fallback site at NORAD headquarters in Cheyenne Mountain. But I think it's safe to say that if any nation comes ashore to invade, they will pay a heavy price. It's that simple. We'll launch counter strikes at their capital so that they have nothing left to return to. We will sink their ships and drown their ambitions. But we also have to survive the domestic attacks from our fellow citizens from D.C. who want a globalist empire instead of the constitutional republic that George Washington and Thomas Jefferson and our Founding Fathers designed."

Levi fishes an American Spirit cigarette from a dwindling pack in his jacket pocket, a pack he picked up at the rest stop in Nashville, lights it, and takes a deep drag before exhaling grey smoke into the wind. He looks out along the tranquil basin below a darkening sky and reaches the palm of his left hand out to catch falling snowflakes. Silently wondering how much of life is a war between books.

"A new existence has been born," Mallory says. "And I want Outlander beside me as we walk into it." Then she stands and steps out onto the plateau to pray for her fiancé.

Levi heads back inside the lodge and washes up in a trough of melted snow before sinking into a rocking chair in the lobby. He shuts his eyes and leans back to rock the chair into a slow, soothing motion, taking long deep breaths in through his mouth and exhaling slowly through his nose to calm his nerves.

"Wake up, Shenandoah." Zulu calls as he walks by with a pack of commandos. "Grab your go bag. We'll be dustin' off soon."

A groggy Levi pushes away fatigue and stretches before walking his soreness outside into the starlight. He slings his machine gun across his chest and moves across the frozen battleground past Outlander's banged up pickup truck where he spots an American flag fluttering on a pole mounted on a corner panel. As he reaches his truck nearby, he looks back and notices two bullet holes seared in the red and white stripes of the flag, the punctures in the cloth resembling fang marks.

Levi locates his rucksack in the floorboard of his truck, unfastens the top and digs down into the gear until he finds his *mezuzah*. He removes the *mezuzah* and binds it on his pack by tying loops of rope through the brushed metal's soldered coils. Then he looks out over the field of snow and watches the moon rise into the faint crimson ion waves of the flaring Aurora Terra as he remembers a world that no longer exists. He peers into the sheer endlessness of the transitioning sky, at pulsing ethereal light ripping apart civilization along invisible wavelengths, and he hopes that the human constellation of Secret Eden will continue to remain alive, and that ultimately, their contributions will survive.

Levi Wolff looks back on an esoteric path that intersected with the saga of Secret Eden. Profound images of his lost year and purging travels form a mosaic that he carries into the unknown. A strange time not yet defined. A vest with two patches of covert identity entering a new dark age with the elusive whisper of life sublime, a whisper that Wisdom was once known by a different name, and her name was Eden.

He stares out across Yellowstone National Park. Just beyond the tree line, he spots a wild wolf pack mashing their way across thick snow. A trailing wolf halts and swivels. Its grey fur coat tight over a muscular frame. Curious yellow and blue heterochromatic eyes peer at him as nostrils flare, trying to detect his scent in the air. Then the wolf tilts its head to the sky and howls the song of a species that is once again free to roam the sacred land alongside the spirit of their ancestors.

THE END